Legends

A Literary Journal from Grey Wolfe Publishing

Spring & Summer 2014

Edited by Diana Kathryn Plopa
and Jennifer Koch

Grey Wolfe Publishing, LLC
PO Box 1088
Birmingham, Michigan 48009
www.GreyWolfePublishing.com

© 2014 Grey Wolfe Publishing
Published by Grey Wolfe Publishing, LLC
www.GreyWolfePublishing.com
All Rights Reserved

ISBN: 978-1628280395
Library of Congress Control Number: 2014947171

Legends

Grey Wolfe Publishing's
Literary Journal
Spring & Summer 2014

Edited by Diana Kathryn Plopa
and Jennifer Koch

Legends is a literary journal produced by Grey Wolfe Publishing.

Four times a year, talented writers from around the globe lend their work to this showcase of short stories, essays and poems for your reading enjoyment.

Some of the stories and poems within these pages may help you revisit memories you thought you'd forgotten. Others may reawaken emotions long dormant. And still others may reacquaint you with the laughter of your childhood. Regardless of which piece of poetry or prose you find most appealing, we are certain that these authors will quickly become some of your new favorites.

Grey Wolfe Publishing is an independent publishing house, headquartered in Michigan. We are committed to walking through the paths of the publishing forest with our authors as equals; never leading, never following... always side-by-side, with the strength and confidence of the Pack.

Ni Bóna Na Coróin.

Acknowledgements

The production of this book each quarter could not be accomplished without the expertise, literary passion and dedication of our amazing Pack. Each is a writer as well as a company team member; and each lends their unique perspective to serve both the company and our authors with integrity and creativity. We are grateful for their daily contributions to the growth of the Pack.

Contents

1.
A Chick in the Fence
A. J. Huffman

Three links down in an empty
expanse of silver rests a nestling.
A fluffy feather non-descript species,
practicing flight. Watch it wobble,
helplessly heralding balance as it braces
its tiny wings. Two flaps and it falters.
Shakily resettles before beginning
again. It gives a furtive quasi-battle cry.
Flap, flap, flutter. Little legs release
their hold on security, and it's up.
Struggling through a breezy headwind
that must feel like a gale force against its beak.
I watch it gain. Air and speed
thrust it higher, further. I can almost feel
it smiling through the ever-growing distance.

2.
A Midsummer's Song
By Sean Padraic McCarthy

He dreamed of fairies. Water nymphs. They weren't very small—they were actually the size of grown women—and they would sing to him. The words of their songs trickling like water, fleeting and distant, and mixing with the sound of the stream that ran in the woods behind his home. Ronan could never hear the stream during the day, only late at night, lying in bed as he drifted off to sleep. One world mixing, merging, with the other. The fairies were often dripping wet, beautiful and blue in the light of the moon, and they would come to his back deck, and sing outside his window. There for a moment, and suddenly gone. Ronan would wake, but Ania never stirred. Never.

It was June, and on Saturday nights they had bonfires in the yard. Flames rising, reaching, into the darkness. Crackling sparks and floating ash. The neighborhood was surrounded by woods, wrapped in green this time of year, and the branches of the trees seemed to wave in the ripples of heat given off by the fires. At other times, in winter, you could see through the trees, into the distance, but not now. Green came from everywhere almost overnight. Ronan loved this time of year.

Ania liked fires, and she liked to build theirs as high as possible. More kindling, more cardboard—corrugated cardboard from cases of wine—anything to make it higher, hotter. Their girls were young, but sometimes on Saturdays Ronan and Ania would let them stay up and swim in the pool, above the ground and water up to their chins. Blowing bubbles through the water each time they went to speak. The next door neighbors' girls were older, all three in college--the mother an artist of some sort and the father gone these past few weeks—and they liked to swim at night, too. Sleep all day, swim all night. One of the girls was engaged, and her father had walked out due to the engagement; he couldn't abide the girl's choice of a husband and the mother stood by her daughter. Other than that, Ronan didn't know much about it. All three were beautiful girls—sleepy eyes and subtle curves, full lips-- looking very much alike except for the color of their hair. Ebony, Auburn, and Blonde. It was the blonde, Eydis, who was engaged to be married. She was the oldest, just graduated from a college in Maine. Sometimes at night, the fire going, and his own girls in the pool, Ronan would watch the neighbors' girls' shadows moving through the yard next door, climbing onto their deck and splashing into their pool.

It was impossible to tell at night whether the girls wore any clothes. Ronan imagined they did, but he liked to think they did not. If anything, they wore nothing more than bikinis, and their bodies, lithe like the branches of trees bending in the wind, were little more than silhouettes. They would disappear beneath the water, and then break open the night again as they splashed to the top. Ania, in the beach chair across from him, a clear gin and tonic beside her, slice of lime floating at the top, would watch him watching sometimes, and sometimes she would ask him what he was watching, and he might smile a little. "I'm not. I'm listening."

The neighbors' girls got their looks from their mother, Freyja, still curved where she needed to be, but crow's feet coming out of the corners of her eyes. Their father, Alva, was large—barrel-chest and hard, round belly—and his head was massive, ringed with a beard. He laughed at what he said, and he laughed at what you said—everything was amusing—and he didn't seem the type to walk out the door. But types changed when doors closed—the walls of privacy both smothering and expanding the personalities within—and if nothing else, Ronan knew this.

The neighbors came from Europe--a Nordic city that was impossible to pronounce—and they started having the bonfires this time of year, waxing towards the solstice, years before Ronan and

Ania followed suit, and Ronan sometimes wandered over there after Ania fell asleep. The fireflies were always out in June and they flashed all about the yard. Ronan had sworn once that he had seen Alva snatch one and eat it.   Twisting his lips and swallowing a little. But then he sipped his beer, and continued on talking; lifting a stick to poke at the fire. Alva's fires were always neat, orderly, while Ronan's and Ania's were always a mess, snapping, tumbling, charred logs and pieces of sticks. Ronan couldn't put an age on Alva, and he was never quite clear on what he did for work.

Communications, the man had said once, but that was all. Not with what, with whom. Ronan worked as a radiologist.

"The thing I don't like about over here," Alva told Ronan once as they stood about the fire, "is the length of the days as the solstice approaches. Much too short. Back home we have a few minutes of darkness, and that's it. And then, in the winter, when it is supposed to be dark, it is, all day long. Gives you plenty of time to crawl away and sleep."

"I hear that's why the rates of depression are so high in that part of the world," Ronan had said, and the man looked puzzled.

"Depression?" he said.   "Well, we don't know much about that." He laughed, smashed his wine tumbler against the rocks, and then clapped his hands and Freyja brought another. One for Ronan, too. Freyja's eyes winged up, curled, on the sides; her lashes were very long. Sleepy and seductive. They were a remarkable blue. A blue you could discern even here in the darkness, by the light of the fire; Ronan found himself mesmerized. Then she smiled a little, and for a second he swore she licked her lips. But she wouldn't be licking her lips, not here, not in front of her husband. Ronan looked down into the pool of his wine, the light of the flame reflecting off the crystal.   He'd had too much to drink.

Ronan had a hard time believing a man who seemed to exert so much control over a household would stay away for long, disenchanted or not with his daughter's choice of husbands; but just a few weeks before he did.   And before he left, he spoke to Ronan on the importance of lineage.

"The bloodline is very important," he said.   He was looking slightly more anxious, slightly less confident.   Alva without his confidence was like a general without his stars.   You could almost see the pride draining from his face, simmering to rage.   "The blood line is everything," he said, "It dictates eternity."

"Eternity?" Ronan asked.

"We need to know who we'll be spending it with.   We need to like them."

"And what if we don't?" Ronan asked.

Alva just looked off towards the moon.   "Well... it can make for a very long time."

Ronan had seen the boy, the fiancé, before.   He walked with his shoulders back and his hips jutted forward, almost as if his legs, as slow as they seemed, were moving faster than the rest of his body.   He always had his thumbs in his pockets. Spiked hair, and a little too much leather.   He looked something like Sid Vicious, Ronan thought.   Ronan had liked the Sex Pistol's music when he was young, but he could never really say he would like to be in a room with Sid Vicious, not without open windows, so maybe Alva was right.   Eternity might look like a very long time.

Ronan smiled at him.   "So you believe in the afterlife?"
"The afterlife?" the man said.   "I believe in life.   Life is life. There, here, then or now." He lowered his head and peered at Ronan.   "You really are a peculiar man."

Ronan returned home that evening, the bedroom blue in the light of the moon, and he had another dream. He could hear singing coming from outside. He sat up in bed, gazed over at Ania. Sleeping on her back, chin raised and lips moving in and out as she blew puffs of quiet air towards the ceiling. Ania was a pretty woman. Slim in frame, with a tiny waist and just enough hips. Her hair was dark and her eyes were blue and alert. Eyes that could kiss you one minute and cut you the next. Ania's entire essence was contained in her eyes. Fragile and explosive. But now she was sleeping, and either she couldn't hear the singing, or Ronan wasn't really hearing it either. It could be so hard to tell this time of night.

He climbed out of the bed, T-shirt and boxers, and went to the door. The door led out to their top deck. A promenade of a deck that spanned the length of the house and had cost more than a few months' pay. The curtains on the window of the door were sheer; Ronan pushed them aside, and squinted out upon the night. He could still hear the singing, now quieter, more distant, but he couldn't see anything except for the empty deck chairs, the black iron table, and an overturned sea shell holding a half smoked cigar. They looked like props from a play in the moonlight, abandoned by the cast and long forgotten. He opened the door, the night air immediately damp and warm, and then he heard laughing.

They were at the top of stairs. One was perched on the rail, leaning back, supporting herself with her hands, long legs folded. Bare. Her entire body was bare, ringlets of wet hair clinging to her forehead and cheeks. And the second one looked as if she were doing a gymnastics act—either walking on her hands on the rail, or clinging to it, holding on so the breeze wouldn't take her away. But there was no breeze, and the fairy's nightgown slipped down, covering her face. The third was floating, resting her head on her hands as she lay on her side. Wide eyed, and smiling. And all were singing, he was sure of it, though none of their lips were moving, and the sound seemed to come from all around. Emanating from the night, the woods and the heavens. Ronan pulled the bedroom door shut quietly behind him. Something pulled him forward, and as it did he could barely feel the deck below his feet. The music had grown louder. He approached the first woman. She looked both completely familiar and completely unfamiliar all at once. He knew her—he knew that he knew her, but in the same instant he was sure he had never seen her before. She smelled of lilacs and moss-- the forest floor--and also of water. The stream. The music was part of the water, mixed with the water, and there was a small smear of green running down her cheek. Algae? Ronan placed his hands on her shoulders. Wet and smooth, delicate. He could feel the other two closing in around him. All three were incredibly close. The one before him parted her mouth, a small drop of water shimmering on her upper lip as she did, and Ronan moved in to kiss her. He was less than a few inches away when her eyes locked wide open. Glass eyes. Lifeless with terror and seeing something beyond him.

Ronan bolted up in bed. His head was damp with sweat. The room was dark, the moon gone. Ania lay on her side, sleeping. The blanket was off, and she had removed her nightgown at some point, naked now. She must have been warm. Ronan lay facing her, tracing a finger down along the side of her ribs and then up and over her hip. After a moment, she mumbled something, and then rolled over, facing away from him.

The next day was Sunday, and she was up before him. Ronan had never been an early riser--always a struggle--and it didn't seem to be getting any better with age. He had always been a night owl. The door flew open, and the girls were scrambling in, eyes alight with mischief, jumping on the bed and climbing in beside him. Eight and six. Brunette and Blonde. Haley and Maeve. Haley with angular features, lean and a wit; and Maeve, round high cheeks, pale blue eyes, the faint glimpse of a wine stain surrounding the right. A few freckles across the nose. Probably the more compassionate of the two, Ronan thought, but it was really too early to tell. They each lay on either side of him, Maeve cuddling up, her head on his chest, and Haley flat on her back. Staring at the ceiling. The fan slowly spinning. Ronan's head was pounding a little. Too much to drink with Alva.

"Mummy says if you don't get up soon, we're going to church without you," Maeve said.

"You can tell Mummy I won't fight her on that," he said.

"Do you want to fight her?" Maeve said.

"Not without gloves," said Ronan.

"Maeve," said Haley. "That's stupid. Boys don't fight girls, and if they did, the girls would always win."

Maeve turned her head, chin on his chest. "That doesn't mean he doesn't want to. Do you want to fight her?"

Ronan took a breath. "Definitely not. Haley is right. Your mother would win."

Maeve put her head back down. "She does have big muscles," she said. Still not looking up, she asked. "What's on your face?"

"What's on my face where?"

She reached up and touched his cheek. "Here."

"I'm not sure," he said, touching the spot. "Maybe it's ash. Ashes from the fire."

Maeve was still staring at the fan, silently singing, and plucking invisible things from the air. Imitating a performer, perhaps. "It's green."

"Green?" he said.

"The stuff on your face," said Haley. "It looks green."

Ronan gently pushed Maeve aside, and sat up. Gazed into the dressing mirror at the foot of the bed. Green. A long, thin streak, running the length of his cheek. Appearing as if it had been drawn with the tip of a finger.

His head hurt worse at church. The delayed hangover. A giddy, silly, sick feeling. Maeve and Haley were singing in the children's choir up on the altar. He loved to see them singing but it made the Mass that much longer, that much more painful. A song between each of the rites. Maeve was just learning to read, so she sang what she memorized by ear, and faked along with the rest. She was even more precious when faking, he thought—her mouth opening and closing like a fish gasping to breathe.

The priest had finished the Gospel and was giving his sermon. Father Dan. Thinning gray hair and thick black rimmed glasses. Italian looking. Short, slim. Ran a tight ship. He was talking about the upcoming Feast of Saint John. Salome first dancing for him, then dancing with him—his head on a plate. The Catholics had corralled the Summer Solstice, Mid-Summer's Night, and made it their own. The Feast for John. His birthday was supposedly exactly six months before Christ's and that was how they said they arrived at the date. Ronan had read that somewhere. They took all the Pagan holidays and tweaked them a bit, out with the heathens and in with the saints. But the priest wasn't talking about that, not about the solstice, the pagans, he was talking about John, and water. Spiritual cleansing. Christ bowed before John, and John made it clear—he had no business baptizing him. But he did anyway. And John was considered a pagan of sorts, wasn't he? A wild man of the woods. Ronan thought back on his dream. The fairies. Had they returned to the woods? He couldn't remember. Just the eyes. Vacant and terrified all of a sudden. Of what?

Ania had her head down. She looked beautiful with her head bowed, eyes slightly shut. Somehow holy. Ania was of Russian descent. Her family had been Jewish at one point, she said, and then some time back, they converted to Catholicism. Or someone converted them. Everyone had been converted at one point or another, Ronan figured, even his own people. The Celts in the woods, way back when . Druid priests. Blood and bones and sacrifice, and then on the Solstice, waiting for the sun. Much beauty and much horror. A grand reflection of life. The pagans were better at reflecting life than the Christians, he figured. The Christians, the Catholics, distorted it the image, the perception, to suit their needs. The pagans absorbed it, gave themselves to it. The energy of the people, plants, soil, and trees. Water. Spirits. All building now. Building to crescendo, and then getting ready to fall. Daylight deteriorating. He hated it when the light began to fade. No way to stop it though. He needed to embrace it. Embrace everything.

The priest took a seat in his big chair, bowed his head in reflection for a moment, and then stood to continue on with the Mass. The Apostle's Creed. And then again the girls were singing.

Ania was in work mode as soon as they got home. Shorts and tank top, hair in a ponytail. Dragging the hose about the yard. There were flowers all over the yard. Roses, Long Island Daisies, Hydrangeas, and Impatiens. Surrounding the trees, in gardens before the front porch, the sides of the house, behind the back deck. Around the little gray shed. And this time of year, the woods looked to be drawing closer and closer. Reaching, breathing. The woods were so thick, everything green. Stand on the edge of the yard. One step and then gone. No one would see you.

He asked Ania the whereabouts of the shovel, but she wasn't easy to talk to when in work mode. She kept moving away from you.

"Probably where you left it," she said at last.

"I thought I left it in the shed," he said.

She pulled the hose, started on the flowers on the side of the house. "Then look in the shed."

"It's not there."

"Well, I don't know what you did with it then."

"I thought maybe you might have had it."

She still hadn't looked at him. It was often impossible to tell what he had done. If he had done anything. Sometimes he did, sometimes he didn't, and it didn't always matter. More often than not there was the sense that he did. She was pissed at him because of what he did. What did he do? Guilt. Irish. Catholic. It flooded the body and clouded the brain, the soul. We were always guilty of something. The church liked you to know that. So did Ania. "Not today," she said. "I haven't seen it. Ask the girls. Maybe they had it."

"Are we still going to the beach tomorrow night?" he asked. "The beach," was actually a fort on a hill above the beach. He had proposed to Ania there on the Summer Solstice twelve years ago, and now each year they went back to celebrate, toast. He proposed with a poem. First and last jaunt into the literary world. It was probably terrible, he figured, but she said she liked it, said she loved it. She lied.

She stopped and looked at him. Mild surprise. "I thought that was the plan," she said, and then she yanked on the hose again; it had kinked, stopping the flow of water. Ania swore, loudly. The goddamn hose. The goddamn hose was a piece of shit. They needed a new one. A heavy rubber one. Not this piece of shit.

Ronan found the shovel lying in the grass near the sandbox and headed over to the shed. They had an arbor leaning against the side. He was planting three grape vines. Red grapes. The vines had been sitting in their pots waiting to be planted for a month. Small, wooden plants. They looked dead. Though grape vines always looked dead before you planted them for some reason. But why wouldn't they grow in the pot, just a little? This time of year, everything grew. Not the grape vines. Stubborn. Grapes would be good though. Home pressed wine. Grape juice dribbling over their chins. Grape juice, and the blood of wild animals. Bacchus. As wild as an animal himself. John the Baptist may have been Bacchus. Someone had thrown that out somewhere. He had read it. But these days you could throw anything out there on the internet. Nothing needed to be legit, nothing needed to be true. Everyone was an expert.

He stepped on the shovel. The earth soft, it slipped right in. Ania was crouching now by her garden. He loved the crouching look. He loved her ass. She had won awards at work for having the best ass, she had told him, one of these days she was going to come home with a trophy, or at least a medal and certificate. She took that sort of thing well. She took pride in her ass. He took pride in her ass. He wanted her ass. But she wouldn't let him near her now. Not while in work mode. She'd stop him right at the gate. Demand to see his papers.

Maeve was coming across the yard. He needed to clear his head. Wasn't good-- having bad thoughts about Ania when the little ones were nearby. Dirty. Dirty old man. Maeve moved, shoulders square, in quick little steps not seeming to touch the Earth. She had a smear of something on her face. Soil. And her hair pulled up in a palm tree.

"Daddy."

"Sweetie." He stepped again on the shovel.

"What are you planting?"

"Grape vines," he said. "Do you like grapes?"

"No," she said. No surprise. Maeve liked nothing. Bagels, pizza, chicken nuggets, and waffles. That was about it. "When are you going to work on our fort?"

The fort. A sad, sorry state of affairs. Ten feet in the air, nestled between the four trunks of an enormous pine tree. Mismatched boards, all different shapes and sizes. Some looking new, some very gray, beginning to rot. The project had been going on since last summer. The problem with the pine tree was the wood was too soft. The nails came out, floors collapsed. He kept having to start over. That wouldn't be good to have them up there when the floors collapsed. His babies barreling to the earth. It would be better to move the fort to the woods, find a new tree. But the problem was, you couldn't see them in the woods, couldn't watch them. Anything could happen in the woods. Anyone could come along. Maybe even Old Scratch himself, covered in soot. Scratch must love the solstice, he figured. Love the pagans. Willingly handing themselves over to him. Witches.

"I don't think the fort is safe up there, honey. I think we need to find a new spot."

"That's just because Belinda was up in it," said Maeve. Belinda was Haley's friend. Same age, twice Haley's size. A little ogre of sorts. He remembered her pushing Haley down in the yard when they were only two. Pushing her down, and standing over her, victorious, daring her to get up. Haley crying. They were always fighting, and then always friends again, but Belinda called the shots. Haley was afraid to act her age—dolls and dress-up and make believe—when Belinda was around, she called her a baby. They were over by the swing-set now. "Belinda breaks everything," Maeve said.

"Well, it doesn't matter who does it," Ronan said. "If it can't hold people, it's not safe. I have to figure something out."

"Belinda said to tell you to do it today," Maeve said.

Ronan looked over at the chubby little girl, swaying back and forth on the swing. Haley had a stick in her hand, talking to her about something, but Belinda didn't appear to be listening; she was staring at Ronan. "Well, tell her I'll get right on it," he told Maeve.

A voyeur. He had gone into the woods after planting the grape vines to take a nap. Out behind the neighbors' house. Into the brush and gone from sight. No-one could see him. He knew it was a dream, something told him it was a dream, and still he wasn't sure. If it were a dream, and he knew it, there should be no fear of getting caught—anything should go--and yet the fear was there. The sun was bright, but barely filtering through the trees, the woods so thick. Puzzle cutouts of blue above him. The neighbor's girls were out in the yard, lying in the sun. Three chairs in a row, all facing the woods. One of them rolled over, up on her hands and knees for a moment, and Ronan felt his heart pick up, everything pick up. And then he felt a hand on his shoulder. He spun around and Alva was there. Towering above him, smiling.

The next day was the solstice, and he got up at dawn to greet the sun. Took a cup of coffee to the deck. The Earth was just coming alive, birds calling, the yard and the deck damp with dew. The sun would dry it all within an hour, but now there was a low mist crawling across the lawn, in and out of the trees. For a second he believed he saw, from the corner of his eye, a man walking through the neighbor's yard, coming from the woods. Alva. But when he turned his head quick there was no one there.

Ronan ate his breakfast and then he took his axe and went to the woods. Wood for the evening's pyre. There wasn't any need to cut down new trees—enough had fallen during the course of the year; Ronan could just cut up what lay on the ground—but he wondered if he did, if he might hear them scream. On this day if any day, he figured, the astral thin, the spirits all active. He wondered if people ever actually believed that trees had spirits or if it just made for good stories. Good for the imagination. The woods was always good for the imagination, it was one thing he loved about it. He found an old, fallen maple—already beginning to show signs of rot—and he began to chop.

They left for sea just after five. A girl from down the street was babysitting. Seventeen. Blonde hair, large breasts, and popping bubbles with her gum. Freckles on the bridge of her nose. Ronan had gone to the yard with his own girls before they left, and had them pick a few flowers.

"If you put a flower beneath your pillow on Midsummer's Night, you'll dream of your future husband," he said.

"Who says?" asked Haley.

"The Swedes," he said. "The Danes."

"The Great Danes?" asked Maeve.

"Yes, them," he said.

"Well," said Maeve, "what do I want to listen to a dog for?"

Ronan looked up. The sky was still very blue, but it was very warm, and this time of year the clouds could roll in quickly. Rumbles of thunder and lightning cutting the sky. He hoped it wouldn't happen. "It depends how smart the dog is."

"Who do you think my husband will be?" asked Maeve. "Do you think it will be Frankie?" Frankie was her friend from school. He drew her pictures. Potato Men. Sometimes with swords, sometimes with guns. Violent potatoes. A rebellion of roots.

"No, I don't think so," he said. "I don't think it will be Frankie."

In the end, Maeve took three daisies, and Haley a couple of impatiens. They still weren't sure if they should believe him, but they seemed excited about the whole thing. It was funny, he thought--you tell the same tale to little boys, and they'd make a face and probably go running. Not little girls.

The beach was close to an hour away. A twenty-minute ride through the peninsula of the town. It was a very pretty town. Small cottages spotting several hills, boats moored in the bay, clam shacks and the old Carousel. He could see the lined trees on the hills of World's End out in the distance. The witches—local wiccans-- used to gather out on World's End on the solstice. He had to remember to look for the fires on the way home.

Ronan and Ania spread a blanket on the ramparts of the fort. Graves clustering the landscape below. The stone tower looming at the summit. The original fort had been used in the Revolutionary War to hold off the British, but that one had been buried beneath a concrete nineteenth century bastion. Now crumbling. The steel rings to hold the cannons still hanging from the walls. Earth and grass covering the ramparts. Graffiti everywhere, and the Boston Light and Graves Light spinning their beacons at the entrance to the harbor.

Ronan uncorked the wine, and Ania spread a plate with bread and cheese. You had to be vigilante, keeping an eye out for the police. The night he proposed they had almost been arrested— the spotlight on them, and bullhorn going. Trespassing, subject to arrest. Ania had flashed the cop her ring though—a blue sapphire, diamond on either side—and he had been good enough to let it slide. Often they didn't, down here.

Now Ania complained that they couldn't see the sun setting. Trees had grown, tall bushes, seemingly out of nowhere.

Ronan tore off a piece of bread. "I don't think we've ever really been able to see it," he said. "Not from this angle, I mean."

"Then why do we come up here?" She was wearing a short, blue wrap around skirt. The blue, the sapphire, her eyes; he loved the skirt on her. He wanted to be inside it with her, take up residence.

"Because this is where I asked you to marry me."

"Well, why did you pick a spot where you can't see the sun set?"

"You can see the lighthouses."

"The lighthouses aren't the sun."

"I thought you wanted to be home by dusk anyway," he said.

"I do."

"Well, then we'll be watching the sun set at home."

They sat in quiet for a few minutes, sipping their wine, and then he leaned over to kiss her. She returned the kiss quick, but then pulled away. Not in public, she said. She used to love it in public, used to tell him he didn't demonstrate affection enough in public. He wanted to now, wanted to roll about in the grass. Lift that skirt above her waist. Demonstrate as much as he could. He tried to kiss her again, again failed.

Before they left they heard a distant barking. Seals were back in the harbor now. All the wildlife seemed to be returning. Less hunting, and fewer places for the animals to go. He wondered if they could be Selkies. Flopping to the beach to shed their skins. Beautiful maidens. This night of all nights, they were supposed to be about.

In the car, he slipped in his Beach Boys CD. *Endless Summer.* Ania sighed. "I hate the Beach Boys," she said.

The girls were in the yard with the babysitter when they finally made it home. They were playing ball. Everything was blue gray. Just a few minutes to sunset. Haley kicked the ball into the woods, and then both she and Maeve ran in to retrieve it, the babysitter running behind them. All three there one moment, then gone the next, reappearing a moment later, almost like a flash of light, his mind playing tricks on him. Maeve had the ball, running with it, and Haley was in pursuit. Haley tackled her, and they rolled about the lawn. The babysitter came out then, a leaf stuck in her hair.

After Ronan drove the babysitter home, they started the fire. The girls stayed with them until they began to nod off, and then he carried them inside. Ronan was beginning to nod off himself. He looked through the flames, the rising ripples of heat. Ania had her legs pulled up under her, her arms pulled tight around her chest. Gazing intently. "Are we going to jump over it?" Ronan asked, gesturing to the fire. "I think we're supposed to jump over it."

She yawned. "You can. I'm not moving."

They had been drinking martinis, each had had two, and now his head felt fogged. He looked up at the sky. Clear. The constellations getting brighter. Then he looked over at the neighbor's yard. No fire tonight. Not with Alva still gone. Not even on the Solstice. The yard was very dark. Just one square of yellow light standing out in the silhouette of their home.

Ronan was soon walking down the path through the woods. Twigs snapping beneath his feet. He turned back to see Ania, still sitting at the edge of the fire. The light from the flames flickering across her cheeks. He couldn't tell if her eyes were open or closed. He contemplated going back, he didn't remember getting up and leaving, but then he felt fingers on his arm, running up the length of it, tickling, and then grabbing firm, and then he heard laughter in his ear. Soft and small but very close. He spun his head around but there was no one there. But now he could see the flames of another fire off in the distance. He didn't know whether to head towards it or return to his own. His gut told him to return, but then once again he felt fingers gripping his arm, invisible fingers, pulling him towards the fire, towards the stream. He could hear soft music, mixing with the sound of the water. A flute of some sort, or perhaps it was a piccolo.

The girls were all about the fire. The girls from next door, and their mother, Freyja. All wearing wreathes of flowers in their hair, and blue eyes sparkling in the light of the flames. And all barely dressed. One topless with a sheer bikini, one wearing nothing more than a second wreath of flowers tied about her waist. And Freyja in a short, sheer dress, nothing beneath. Everything visible.

Only Eydis wore a dress that wasn't sheer; it had a triangular neckline that reached her navel, exposing the sides of her breasts. The skirt was short, cut high on the thigh, cinched with a belt, making her appear as if she stepped out of a Grecian myth. The flowers in her hair were white; the flowers in the hair of the others were blue.

The fire had been built in the middle of three concentric circles of stones, the ones on the outer circle were very large, the stones of the other two consecutively smaller, but all still large enough to stand out in the woods. Ronan had been out here several times. He wondered how he could have missed them.

The two younger girls approached Eydis, fastening flowers to her dress, whispering in her ear, giggling and then looking back at Ronan. The one only wearing the wreath about her waist leaned over as she whispered, and Ronan felt his head begin to spin, his heart to pound. Then, in an instant, she was beside him, taking his hand and putting it to her breast, her eyes alight and her ears pointier than he had ever seen them. Not in the yard, not in dreams. And then she was gone again, a flash. Freyja walked over then, or glided, as it seemed her feet were not touching the Earth, and she placed her hands on his shoulders. "I am so happy you came," she said. She tilted her face forward, kissing him lightly, and then when he opened his lips, a quick flick of the tongue.

She drew back, puzzled. "You don't like to be kissed?"

"You're married," he said, trying to control his thoughts, his hands. "Alva."

Freyja pursed her lips, shook her head. "That does not matter. Not on a wedding night, not on the solstice. On a wedding night, how do you say? ...anything goes. As soon as we conclude the ceremony, you can have any one of us." She kissed him quickly again, and then shook her finger. "Except for the bride. The law says you cannot touch the bride, to touch the bride would be very, very bad." She moved in closer, her arms about his neck now, her body pressed tight against him, warm, wonderful and firm, and then one of the girls had their finger beneath his chin, turning his head and pressing a wooden chalice to his lips. It was something like wine, but sweeter. Cold and delicious. And the girl was floating, he was sure of it.

"If you have second thoughts," she said, "this will erase them."

"Is that good?" he whispered.

She nodded. "That's very good." She took his hand again. Freyja was now back on the other side of the fire, and Eydis had taken a seat in a tall wooden chair. A throne bedecked in wreaths of white flowers, and smothered in ivory, an identical throne, slightly larger, stood empty next to her.

It was then that the boy appeared at the foot of the path that meandered into the darkness. A path in the opposite direction from which Ronan had come from. The boy with spiked hair. The groom. His pupils looking so dilated, he seemed in a trance, or possibly drugged, and his hands were shaking. Freyja raised a finger and beckoned him towards her. The boy wore no shirt, and he had a strange marking painted across his chest. A symbol. A circle with three tapering lines inside, moving towards each other, topped with three dots. The boy started towards Freyja, and Eydis watched in anticipation as he did. The drink had gone further to Ronan's head and the colors of the night, reflecting off the fire, seemed more pronounced now. Pulsing, breathing. He was suddenly struck with the feeling that he had been here before, that this had happened before, déjà vu, but of course he hadn't. It hadn't.

As soon as the boy reached Freyja, Eydis stepped down from the throne. The other girls had disappeared, hovering in the background, and the music had grown louder. Freyja leaned over to whisper in the boy's ear, and then, smiling, she took his hand and placed it in Eydis's. The boy still looked terrified, but Eydis looked completely at ease. Freyja stepped away from them, and then stepped behind Eydis. Undoing her robe first at the belt, and then at the neckline. The robe fell to the earth, and then Eydis, now completely naked, stepped closer to her fiancée.

Freyja looked across the fire, beckoning to Ronan. She seemed smaller somehow, and she almost looked a grayish-blue. Mixing with the air, the night. "We need a witness," she whispered, but her lips didn't move, and Ronan started around the fire. He had almost reached the three of them when the vibrations began beneath his feet. Ronan stopped, listening to the sounds coming from the woods. The vibrations were instantly louder, sounding as if they came from an enormous drum, and then his own body was shaking. As were the others. Eydis and the groom were still locked with one another's eyes--the groom still looked unaware of where he was, who he was—but Freyja looked nervously out towards the woods. The sound louder, closer, and now the thumping was followed by the sound of snapping brush. Branches. Trees.

Freyja wet her lips. "Bastard," she hissed out into the night.

Then the spell was broken for Eydis. "Don't let him ruin it!" she shouted at Freyja. She flung her body at the groom, clinging tightly, and then the other two girls were at Ronan's side, clinging.

Ronan looked at the middle one, puzzled.

She nodded. "Daddy," she said. The earth thumped again then, and the three lost their balance, the girls toppling over. A shadow moved over the fire. Freyja was at the edge of the clearing now, hands on her hips, waiting. She didn't need to wait for long. A gigantic limb came swinging out of the darkness, causing the women all to scatter, and sideswiping the groom, sending him sailing into the night. Eydis reappeared again for a moment, and then went flying after him. Freyja was popping in and out, all around the fire, screaming. The limb swung again, and Ronan crouched low to the earth. He looked up to see Alva, wine chalice in one hand—wine wet on his lips--and the limb in the other. His face in a rage, and his eyes on fire, he was as enormous as the trees.

Ronan opened his eyes. Down on his hands knees at the edge of the yard, the edge of the woods, the dew of the grass wet beneath him, and sweat still warm on his brow. He turned back to the woods to see how far he was from the fire, from Alva, but he could see nothing. The night was quiet except for the crickets. He looked at his forearms, smeared with soot, and then pulled something free from his cheek. Pine needles. He looked at his wrist to check the time, but his watch was gone. He wondered how long he had been sleeping. How drunk he had been.

The fire was still going below his back deck, but was now reduced to cinders, and there was no sign of Ania. The chairs all empty. Ronan stumbled through the yard to the stairs to the top deck. The lights in the house next door were all out, and there were no cars on the road. When he got to the top deck, he turned again to the woods, but still there was nothing. He thought of his own fire again, and contemplated hosing it down, but his muscles hurt as did his head, and he just wanted to sleep. Contained in the pit, chances were slim that it would spread.

He reviewed the dream again his head, and started to laugh a little—he would hear about it from Ania, walking off to piss and passing out in the woods. It was the best night of the year, his favorite, and here he had passed out, missed most of it. Ronan slipped off his shoes, and had nearly reached the door to his bedroom when he saw the faint light emanating from inside. Blue.

He pushed open the door. The moon was shining in the window, and everything in the room looked the same. Except for Ania.

Ania was hovering above the bed, her chin resting on the knuckles of her hand. And Ronan felt his breath halt in his lungs. She was looking at him curiously, the way she sometimes did, but her eyes now turned up at the corners, and then there was the thing with her ears. Pointed. Making her possibly more beautiful than she already was.

"Is Oberon all done out there?" she asked.

"Oberon?" Ronan whispered.

"Oberon. Alva. Or whatever he's calling himself now." She sighed. "He's such a boor. A complete ass."

"An ass?"

"An ass," she said, laughing a little. "Speaking of which, what do you think of mine?" She raised her bottom up high, tapped it lightly, playfully. "Shut the door," she said; "will you? Then come on over here so we can have sex."

"Sex?"

"I'll come down," she said.

Ronan swallowed his breath. "Promise?"

Ania nodded. "I promise."

Ronan shut the door, sealing off the night. Then he lay beneath her, his hands pulling her close and securing her to the Earth.

3.
A Spring Afternoon
Dennis Klotz

Lana's alarm clock went off, and she felt fatigued already. She ached and was still a little sleepy but she knew she only had an hour to make Emily breakfast and get her ready for school. She had hoped her allergies weren't as bad, but when she saw Emily's red watery eyes and heard her light voice muffled and deepened by her plugged nose, Lana knew she would have to call the school to tell them Emily wouldn't be in that day, and set another appointment with the pediatrician. Spring meant flowers and playful afternoons at Nana's house, both of which Emily loved, but it also meant allergy season, and this year the pediatrician had told Lana that the pollen would be worse for Emily after such a harsh winter.

They waited for a long time to get in, and on the car ride back after the appointment Emily's nose was runny and there were used tissues already falling out of her pockets onto her booster seat. "I hate this," she said in between sniffles. "I wish I were dead."

"Don't say that honey. That's a very bad thing to say," Lana told her, focusing more on the traffic. "You should never wish you were dead."

"Why? You said fishy was dead."

"I know, but we talked about this." Lana was annoyed, though she tried not to show it.

"Why did he die?"

"That's what happens sometimes. We talked about this," Lana said. "You're giving mommy a headache."

"I miss fishy," Emily pouted.

"I know you do sweetie." Lana said. "I know."

Emily didn't say anything, just sniffled some more and rested her head against the seat belt, looking out the window. "Can we go to Nana's today?"

"Maybe tomorrow, you need your rest."

"But I want to play in the garden."

"It will make your nose worse."

"Please?" Emily pleaded between sniffles.

Lana didn't say anything for a while but she knew Emily loved going to Nana's, even though her cats and her garden made her eyes water if she was there for too long. But Lana needed a break, and she knew it would be good for both of them. "Do you promise to be good?"

"Promise," Emily said.

"Just for a little bit. You need your rest."

Emily napped the rest of the way, and when Lana pulled the car into Nana's driveway, she woke up and smiled.

"I feel better already," she beamed.

Nana greeted them at the door, and Emily ran up and hugged her legs. Lana had called ahead to tell her they were coming for a short visit. When they were inside, Emily went and petted the cats and sat on the floor playing with her toys and stuffed animals she had left there, while Nana went to retrieve some candy to give to her. Nana always had candy to give Emily.

"You spoil her too much," Lana said.

Nana just smiled, "It's only right."

"Can I play outside Nana?" Emily asked.

"Sure, let's go outside. It's too beautiful to be inside."

"It's not good with her allergies; to be outside like that," Lana said.

"Let her play a little bit. She's probably tired of being stuck inside all winter anyway."

Emily was already skipping through the yard when Lana sat down next to Nana on the porch.

"It's so nice out. Spring is such a lovely season." Nana said.

Lana did think it quite nice out, though Nana's garden, redolent of the fresh blooms, smelled more fragrant than usual. "It is."

"You look tired, dear."

Lana leaned forward in her chair and sighed. "I've just been stressed that's all. She's been driving me nuts lately. Between her schoolwork, and her allergies, and all of her questions... it's too much sometimes." She massaged her temples. "Maybe I'm just getting old. I can feel it in my bones. It's not like being thirty anymore."

Nana didn't say anything, just looked at her with her tender eyes. "What?" Lana asked, running her fingers through her hair.

"I would give anything to be your age again. It's such a blessing to be young." Lana didn't know what to say. Nana looked at her for a long time as if seeing beyond her, or deep inside her. Then she looked back at Emily. She was waving to Nana from the garden and Nana waved back to her.

"She's getting big. I could watch her play all day."

"Yeah, she is," Lana said. "Sometimes I guess I forget that they grow up."

"We all do. That's how it is. Always has been."

Lana was speechless again. She looked at Emily, skipping around. She had her same bright hair, and it looked more golden in the sun. She never noticed how beautiful it looked in the sunshine. It almost seemed to sparkle. They sat in silence for a moment, listening to Emily laughing and playing.

"You're expecting, aren't you?" Nana asked.

"How did you know?" asked Lana, her eyes wide now, shocked by her mother's prescience.

"A woman knows these things. You've been acting different the past couple of weeks. Have you told him yet?"

"No," Lana said looking away. "I haven't told anyone."

Lana looked out to where the girl was playing. Nana looked too.

"She's a beautiful girl."

"Yes," Lana said. "So beautiful."

"Just like you were at that age."

Lana felt a heaviness in her, and her eyes began to water like Emily's had earlier.

Nana looked out at Emily playing in the garden. She heard her laugh caught in the gust, and she saw her golden hair flitting in the warm wind as she skipped among the garden, purple and green and gold in the spring afternoon. "That's one thing the world will never run out of," Nana said looking out again at the child in the garden. "Young life."

4.
Across the Silent Distant Sea
Stanley Noah

You see. I'm standing at the window looking out
while in the moment the mirror must see my
reflection. Three of us---window, mirror, me and
the landscape, and lighthouse beyond. You came
in beside me. And we viewed the distant *sea*, the
lay of tides like then-and-there like now-and-here.
The displacements no matter stay. You can see far
away as well as me. You and me in the same *room*,
three dimensional, French doors, the mirror looking
on, window cracked. Once again you standing there
alone like a lamp of fire when I'm gone and return.
You standing here and the sea and the mirror near
the coffee table with flowers and yellow fruit, dark
chocolate and drifting memories. *You*, beside the
window like a painting above in the room of French
windows and the silent sea.

5.
Apple Picking
Chloe Vider

Apple picking
while chickens dance, as though they are walking on hot coals
their pecking beaks opening to shout warnings as
their feathers fall through the air like raindrops
we pick out three ripe red Macintoshes.

Before apples had brand names
and chickens had cages
there was a time of year when you could grow
   'most anything'
eating ripe peaches on the door stoop
watching trees bend in the wind
and children run for cover.

Their muddy sneakers and
a salamander
poking his shy head out of a pocket.

Now the plants are withered
the ground is black underfoot
cracked in every direction
as though the soil has been pulled from all sides
and fallen in on itself trying to find its way back home
behind the old shed there are some
bird corpses and apple cores
  but not a ripe peach in sight.

6.
Backward, Turn Backward
Stanley Noah

Quiet in this square, stained wall-paper room, haunting low-toned
mirror and slow moving music dancing out the short band
radio.   My
mind seems easily to walk backwards the steps of years.
Then profoundly

reality is repeating my personal history
I lived through

7.
Bayonet
Chloe Vider

If you had a bayonet
could you wield it in an energy-saving capacity?
Sluicing through the air and creating wind power?
Holding the weapon in your hands
and finding in it salvation?

Most men cannot.

They are tasked with the impenetrable duty
of watching time tick by as they do Nothing.
The weight of that *nothing* can be Massive
more draining than Atlas's duty
continents digging into his shoulder blades
oceans dripping salty sweat down his forearms.
 Would you drop the whole writhing mess into the depths of space?
Or sacrifice eternity to hold onto
  squabbling men
forgotten arts?

8.
Beginnings
Jay Dardes

Bunny rabbit on a field of grass,
Tender young new shoots.
Winter has been black and necrotic;
We shall live again.
The days of ice were like a held breath;
Pipe now while we dance.

9.
Central Park in the Rain
A. J. Huffman

Poet's Walk ripples in reflection
of leafless trees and empty benches.
Everything runs
for cover from contact with contaminated
precipitation.   I wander alone and umbrellaless,
surprised I am the last
pen holder standing, recording
the truth that can only be found
in momentary spaces
between the drops.

10.
Egged
Evelyn Zimmer

"We are all the Goddess's creatures" the voice behind me said. At least that is how I remember it.

It was one of the summers at our family's estate near Tawnybreeze, before the Scourge, in the time simply known as before. The Bloodstrider's often hosted summer retreats, as was the case with most Nobles of Quels' Thamar. Alaxia was busy helping our mother entertain the Ladies on the far side of the hill, underneath the shade trees, where the mana worms liked to play. The babies, Czarrina and Bellascar were stuck in the nursery with the noble's children of similar age.

Dianna and I had escaped our duties for a magical afternoon of tormenting the cousins, Ceafo was somewhere nearby, her nose in a book as always. Young Thamarian women of that time and class, not quite adults, but old enough to make those near to question if we were, in fact, old enough. After all, to be around the adults, received a rather spectacular education of intrigue; manipulation; seduction; power struggles; intimidation... and if you paid attention, the true mechanics of politics.

We should have been with our mother and Alaxia... hell; we should have been entertaining the others of our age. Somehow, if there was a way for Dianna to be tempted out of doors, she found a way. Being a protective sort, I naturally went with her.

That particular afternoon was no different than most lazy summer afternoons. Breezy, sunny, all of nature robed in her lush glory. Then there was Dianna, her bow slung over her shoulder, stalking a young Golden Hawk through the trees. She was really only after the eggs, what better weapon to use against a male cousin after all, than to egg him from afar? Not wishing to get egged myself; I wisely kept my mouth shut about her activities, pretending to not know where she was, should we happen across anyone.

This continued on for nearly an hour when Father and his cronies came around the bend just as Dianna disappeared; leaving me to smooth things over just in case we were in trouble again, or rather, as always.

They were deep in conversation about the hunt that was to take place the next morning, which was when I heard him: the elder son of a minor neighboring noble. He seemed to be spouting off about the barbaric nature of the hunt and how the tables are stacked against the poor creatures. "Typical" I thought to myself, "arrogant mana-sucking pampered useless little..." was my second thought that got interrupted as I backed farther away from the path into the shadows of the trees and shrubbery to avoid being seen. It was just breezy enough that day to cover the sounds of our movements. I looked above me to the lower limb of a rather stately tree where Dianna raised her finger to her mouth in a gesture for silence.

That is when I saw it, the ivory oval in her hand, just large enough to comfortably fill her palm from the look of it; she bounced it from one palm to the next rather like a juggler might, pure wickedness glinting in her eyes. I attempted a scowl, trying to silently plead with her not to do it, hoping all the while that she would.

My back was to Father and his assembled friends as they continued on just mere feet away, oblivious to the danger about to befall them. Looking Dianna in the eye, I gave into my own wickedness and grinned at her.

"Don't tempt me Eva..." she giggled, nearly giving us away.

"Just don't hit Father" was all I had to say. From her pocket, Dianna withdrew a small sling shot, setting the egg in place; she slowly crouched on the limb above me causing the limb to groan. I froze; sure we would be caught then and there.

I didn't dare turn to look; any movement would catch Father's keen vision. I could hear Dianna trying not to breathe just as the breeze picked up again and saved us. Sometimes, it was good to be a friend of the elements.

The pompous spawn of our neighbor continued in his discontent of having being forced outdoors, let alone to attend the hunt. His whining made me silently hope he was Dianna's target. That was when it happened.

"We are all the Goddess's creatures" the voice behind me said. He was closer than I thought.

"Which is why some of us are predators." I couldn't help it, I swear. It just slipped out. Loud enough to be heard by all, I'm afraid.

I could hear him turn towards me just as Dianna let go of the taught band. The egg hit him square in the forehead. A better shot could not have been made. The timing of movement, the cooperation of the breeze temporarily moving the leaves from Dianna's sight...we were blessed. Dianna leaped from her limb and caught the next one, quickly out of sight and I assumed her to be still nearby.

I stepped forward, knowing there was no getting out of it. Moving the branch of the shrub hiding me, I stepped lightly as if coming from a nature walk and happening upon the conversation innocently.

I stopped short as I nearly collided with him, looking up into his face, for he was much taller than I. "Oh, natural selection in progress, I see." I smiled innocently, an impish tug to my lips. "Father" I nodded to him as I saw him trying to scowl at me, yet the wink he gave me belied his public anger.

"I am sorry gentlemen for interrupting your conversation; it is one near and dear to my heart." I took in the assembled group as I curtsied low; the practice in seductive distraction was not lost on me. I stayed low a fraction longer than necessary, which caused an eye or two to linger. A cough from one of the gentleman, and after a muffled comment from one or two of the gentlemen, a hand offered to bring me up from the curtsey; pleasantries were exchanged.

Mild flirting ensued as the men were laughing at the young noble getting egged and trying to figure out if I was the culprit. Not wishing to accuse a Lady, and their extended hostess of such actions, they made a show of beating about the bushes looking for the means of such an assault on them.

Egg boy was wiping the goo from his red indignant face; sputtering about getting even. No one was paying much attention. Secretly, I think they enjoyed his discomfort themselves.

"Lady Eva, why are you out here alone?" Father asked me, just as Ceafo came bustling around the corner, saving my ass once again.

"Not alone Father, Ceafo and I were simply taking a walk on this lovely afternoon, having just parted ways with Dianna. I believe she went to help in the nursery..." the two of us smiling like angels knowing all the while that we would be getting justice served to us later.

"Better head back up to the hill and see if your Mother needs anything, dear." Father said to me; giving me an opportunity to avoid getting myself in deeper.

"Lady Evalinne, will you be joining the hunt tomorrow?" the boy's father asked.

"Aye, if Father will let me. I'm sure my sisters, Alaxia and Dianna would love to be included." Hope sprang eternal in my young girl's heart as I glance at Father who in turn, promptly acted like he didn't hear me.

"Gentleman, it would appear we should be careful about upsetting our winged creatures. Their opinion of tomorrow's hunt has been well-noted." Father tried to smooth things over as some of the men started to continue on up the path.

As I turned to take Ceafo's arm and begin going back to find Mother, I noticed Father's attention lingered on me. I saw a thoughtful smile play about his lips and his eyes crinkle just the barest amount. I heard him chuckle the words "Predators indeed".

That was the afternoon I remember first, whenever I think of Father.

11.
For Which We Live
Jay Dardes

The storm god swept down from the north
and raped and laid waste without foe—
until now.
The dark lord raged at will and spread sorrow
so that fear and liquor replaced our laughter,
until a crow called,
signaling that the earth would yield no more,
sending forth the black bird as trumpeter of war:
it would fight now.
The ice prince hurled his worst, vicious waves unrelenting,
and we felt and bled but stood, for we must.
And we win.
I see he retreats, I see he weakens, knows fear.
And I see our army that routs him even now.
Our proud army
advancing, so powerful, young, and strong:
this furry rabbit with his leaf of grass.

12.
Grandpa Fella Storyteller
By Jon Moray

I was eight years old when my grandfather died of a sudden heart attack in his wooden rocking chair that was situated beside the fireplace in his living room.

My earliest memory of my grandfather, Grandpa Fella Storyteller, was at five when my parents dropped me off at his country home for the day, while they attended a wedding. I called him Grandpa Fella because he would always call my dad and any other man 'Fella.' He affectionately referred to me as 'Little Fella.' That day I was introduced to his wonderful stories of fantasy and science fiction; time travel was his passion. It was then when I added the 'Storyteller' part to his nickname.

He noisily settled in his chair and motioned me over with a pointed crooked forefinger protruding from his bony hand. A skeleton of a frame, with white, stringy hair, bi-focal glasses, flannel shirt, and jeans with patches on both knees was probably the best way to describe his appearance.

I hopped beside him in his seat that easily accommodated the both of us with room to spare. He thumbed through a loose leaf binder where his hand-written stories were housed and asked me if I wanted to hear a fantastic tale. I nodded with excitement as if I was a bobble-head doll. That day, he told a story about a boy that traveled back in time by spinning a coin counterclockwise to the year that was on the coin. I closed my eyes and the words that floated from his raspy voice guided me along on this fantastic journey. All the while, Grandpa Fella rocked the chair gently as if mimicking a spaceship battling subtle turbulence.

"Someday, I'm going to publish my stories and give books to all of my grandchildren," he said, with eyes that sparkled as if he saw his book-writing dream in my eyes.

"Why don't you use the computer to write, Grandpa Fella Storyteller?"

"I've never learned how to use those things. Besides, I enjoy the scratchy sound the pencil makes when it touches the paper."

From that day on, every visit with Grandpa Fella included a time traveling story in his rocking chair that seamlessly segued into a spaceship when he was deep in his moving narrative. I struggled with the news of his departure. We had made quite a bond.

My parents and I arrived at his home that featured a deep wrap-around porch that sheltered the home from the boiling heat in the heart of summer. I exited the family sedan, leading the way through the front door and my scampering progress into his living room came to an abrupt halt when I saw Grandpa Fella's rocking chair.

As my parents sifted through important papers and remnants in his bedroom, I hurried to the chair as my way of paying homage to my grandpa. My momentum and clumsiness rocked the chair backward and almost upended. I exhaled deeply, allowing my loving memories of Grandpa Fella to swirl in my head. I closed my eyes and imagined him opening his binder, clearing the lingering saliva from his throat and uttering the first word of a highly anticipated tale. Suddenly, I heard his voice, no longer raspy, but clear. I opened my eyes to find only me in the vicinity.

"Close your eyes and enjoy the adventure," said Grandpa Fella, in a soft, reassuring tone, as my startled, rapid heartbeat simmered. I did as instructed as he began to spin a story of a man that was unexpectedly thrust into the future by way of a revolving door serving as a portal. The chair began to rock gently as he described peaceful aliens inhabiting Planet Earth and sharing secrets to a blissful planet. His craft of literary imagery flowed as his creation of well-intended aliens with elongated multi-colored heads and distorted slender bodies made me wish I could travel to that faraway place. I could see his worldly vision as if his ghostly thoughts were remotely transmitted into my brain.

"The end," Grandpa Fella Storyteller announced theatrically, with the promise of more stories as long as I occupied his magical chair. Stories that deserved to be heard and published.

I opened my eyes as my mom approached.

"What's going to happen to Grandpa Fella's easy chair," I asked, expecting an unfavorable answer.

"Grandpa wrote a will about a year ago. In it he said his rocking chair was to go to you. Your father and I discussed the matter and we decided the chair is way too big to keep in your room, so it will be kept in the basement. It's an old and beat up piece of furniture. Are you sure you want it?"

My mother looked at my freckled face and saw Grandpa's youthful enthusiasm in my deep blue marble eyes and crescent moon shaped smile. It was the same demeanor that glossed Grandpa Fella Storyteller's face whenever he discovered a new fantastic story idea.

"I'll take that as a yes," she said, as she lovingly stroked my hair.

As I grew older and the challenges of adulthood and responsibility increased, Grandpa Fella Storyteller's chair collected dust in the basement. I moved out of my folk's home, married, bought a house, and was an expectant father.

My wife had begun her third trimester when she announced her desire for a rocking chair to soothe the baby inside of her and eventually, after the birth. She told me she saw one that caught her eye on one of the shopping channels. Thoughts of Grandpa Fella's chair rocketed back to me like one of his stories. I told her I would look into a chair, grabbed the keys to my SUV, and sped over to my parents' home.

After typical kiss-on-the-cheek pleasantries with my mom, I informed her I would take the rocking chair home with me. A melodically enhanced 'halleluiah' echoed from her vocal chords as I hurried down the creaky basement steps. The chair was draped in an old bed sheet. I stripped away the linen and was floored by the refurbished, solid oak finish that gleamed under the fluorescent lighting.

"Your father and I were going to surprise you with it at the baby shower. I remember that chair being like a best friend to you and thought restoring it would make a great gift. But since the new mommy has a furniture craving, I say you take it now."

I thanked her with a bone cracking, bear hug embrace that would make a chiropractor proud. I carried the chair to my vehicle and carefully placed it inside. I got home and instructed my wife to cover her eyes as I positioned the chair in our living room.

"Okay, you can look now," I said, with anticipation.

She joyfully gasped and covered her mouth in euphoric laughter as I guided her to the chair.

"The baby has been uneasy and kicking up a storm this whole week. I can really use the easy motion now."

She slowly sat down and wiggled herself into maternal comfort. She breathed deeply as her eyes slowly closed like a theater curtain. She smiled as she gently rubbed her belly and I can only wonder if Grandpa Fella Storyteller had begun to narrate a wondrous tale to my little one inside.

13.
Impressions
Dennis Klotz

There are some people who create a mystique about themselves that even the ones closest to them are barely perceptive of the elusive subtleties and the slow and tempestuous oscillations within their personality which come to render the portrait of a person. To the ones in their inner circle, and to those who orbit outside of it, they offer glimpses, fragments and masks, but their true core remains veiled and hidden.

Damien Arthur Roth was in this way a chameleon, with shifting personas which were so carefully refined and suited that no one, save for the rare perceptive individual one may cross paths with once or twice in a lifetime, could have discerned him from the other self which was his truer essence.

The life that had been handed down to him was vast and ripe with opportunities for he had grown up well-off and in a stable household where discipline and ambition were instilled in him at an early age. In his formative years, his father who was well known in circles of finance and business had taught him the ways of the world and the workings of money and wealth. He taught him how to pick trades, how to pick friends, and in his privileged upbringing, Damien grew to expect things which were foreign to other kids. He began to cultivate a mindset that was different from theirs, and when they did not share his worldview, he thought himself apart. He grew to guard these differences out of fear that they would alienate him and out of fear that they would be used against him in one way or another. His father's words were fresh in his mind in those moments. "Keep your cards close to the vest. Watch what you say and what is being said about you," he would tell him. "You are the only one who is able to hurt yourself Damien. Never forget that," he would say; and Damien would say "Yes sir."

He stifled emotions, sensitivities, failings, criticisms, and all things which did not align with the grand way in which he came to view himself. He learned quickly how to spot the weaknesses in people and how to manipulate their shortcomings, but he never viewed this as a negative trait; rather he assumed it was just the natural order of things. No one was without flaws and he even saw his father's conservative rigidity and discipline as a system of outdated values which kept in check all the vices which, coming into his twenties, he was eager to partake in and gorge.

At twenty-one he had hard masculine features and jet black hair that shined blue under the right light. He wore expensive clothes that draped over a body he spent perfecting six days out of the week at dawn; and the way he walked, held a drink, and entered a room, all assured people of his importance and status. Though he was well acquainted with the affluent families of his father's friends, as well as the ones who orbited them –he learned at a young age that money drew people with varying degrees of awe and envy– he found himself drawn to a crowd that was different than his own; one that challenged his perceptions and offered new ideas, and he looked to them as a contrast, for they valued in a way he found remarkable, the things he had not had to struggle for.

He took to stocks and real estate after his father and made a profit regardless of whether the market was bullish or bearish. His work ethic mirrored the way he went about the rest of his life; fast, aggressive and without hesitation or doubt. He apologized for nothing; and the few regrets he had he kept to himself, mostly. He prided himself on amassing in a few years, a large sum of money that allowed him to live in a sizable loft in a trendy part of downtown where the view looked out over Woodward Avenue and he had access to the bustling hub of the weekend nightlife.

His name and reputation preceded him wherever he went, and even the circles he didn't run in seemed to expect and welcome his presence with enthusiasm whenever he made friends with the important people in them. He had a dimorphic and lusty character and there was a robust smolder to his countenance that broke people out of their shells. He was bold, audacious, and frequently found himself at the center of groups; in short amounts of time, he rose to the top and became the link between many other circles. It was through large groups that he remained abreast of the best parties, the fashionable clubs, and whom to take to what place and when. Nights downtown were always a blur of many things; drinks, music, and the shared experience of friends from many different crowds. Detroit in the night time was different than in the day, and when the sun went down there was a new pulse to it. The city came alive then, and there was always a bar or a club or a party to go to. It was through one of these riotous parties that Desiree entered into his life.

II.

Accounts differ among friends on the exact year they met, since the party was drowned out in a sea of other festivities; and those too, all seemed to be lost in the haze of those wild years. It had been a hot night towards the end of spring when Damien had met his friends downtown. The decline in previous decades had forced businesses out of the city, and the people along with it. What remained was a decaying shell of its former greatness, and it attracted young eager types who flocked to it from the surrounding suburbs, some with grand idealizations that they could save it; the other half viewing it as nothing more than a playground in which they could romp and then forget about for five days out of the week. On weekends and on holidays they descended in droves to the city, all of them intoxicated on the promises the night held.

The party he had met Desiree at was not advertised, and the invitation was word of mouth only. The location shifted from warehouse to warehouse in some forgotten part of the city on the last Saturday of the month to avoid suspicion or detection. It began at midnight but it was not until hours later that most people arrived, and it was well into the night when it was in full swing. The hours passed by in a fevered brilliance, and the music and the crowd became one moving beast. The whole underground that populated it became one large community and Damien was moving from group to group through the crowd, drink in hand, a diabolical grin on his face, when he noticed her.

She was talking to her friends, on the edge of the crowd towards the back. There was a quiet intensity to her demeanor which intrigued him. His brain was already humming from several drinks earlier, and when he made conversation with her, his words slipped off of his tongue effortlessly, and with greater frequency. He mistook her indifference for sincere interest and thought he was charming her with his high talk when he excused himself for a moment, only to come back to find her gone. He was not accustomed to being denied anything, least of all women, and he wrote her off as some sort of anomaly and continued on in his hedonistic way, to make the night one to remember –in fragments, for if he didn't remember parts– he would ask a friend the next day to fill in the gaps, and they would laugh and Damien would say with a sly smile,

"You know how I am."

Another hour passed in what felt like five minutes, and things began to wind down. He saw fewer people that he recognized and he realized that many had already left. He was searching the place, trying to gather up his friends to leave when he spotted her heading towards the exit. He walked over to her.

"I was looking for you. I thought you disappeared."

"Yeah I'm taking my friends home. It was nice meeting you."

"Nice meeting you too. You seem cool. Like someone I should get to know." They exchanged numbers.

"Are you free next weekend?"

"I have to see. I'll let you know."

"I'm Damien by the way."

"I know, you told me. I'm Desiree."

She postponed seeing him for two weeks, and he began to think her a lost cause until she finally agreed to meet him on a warm Friday at the museum. It was early evening and he was seated on a bench in the lobby when he saw her. Her dark hair and her dark eyes matched her black dress and all of it hit him at once. Things stirred in him. She looked more magnificent in the light, and from this point on, each time he saw her she seemed to grow more radiant than the time previous. It was this very vitality that she aroused in him, and wore at her reticence and eroded away the walls she had put up until she forgot them all together, and surrendered to the enormous presence of him.

They strolled through the museum, admiring art that was modern, or renaissance or impressionist. He talked in a calm confident manner which set her at ease, and she warmed up to him as they conversed. He inquired about her interests, her past and her future. He wanted to know all of her right then, but he resisted the temptation to dive head first into her life story, or reveal the intimate parts of his own. She was studying graphic design, and the avidity and passion with which she talked about art impressed him. She painted, and she sang sometimes but hadn't in a while. She liked Rembrandt, but preferred impressionist to baroque in art and in music. Their conversation rose and fell like waves on a shore. Damien was walking ahead, his eyes and mind in another place when he realized she had stopped. She was standing in front of a self-portrait of Van Gogh. He stood behind her and looked at it too. She studied it for a long time.

"It's so interesting to see how he viewed himself. He looks sad in this one. So serious, so intense. He painted so many self-portraits. This one he painted this in summer. God, can you imagine summer? In Paris at that time? It must have been beautiful. Absolutely beautiful."

"It must have been nice."

"No one ever realized his genius or his beauty. But he did. He saw it. It's sad no one else saw it though. They see it now, but it's not the same. Not many are recognized in their own time." She looked away a little embarrassed. "I'm sorry, I'm rambling."

"No, no; I was enjoying it. His style is very interesting. What's your favorite painting of his?"

"All of them. I can't pick just one. I love the way he paints, the way he sees things."

"I like him too."

They toured the galleries for forty-five minutes before dining in an upscale establishment a few blocks away where the wine lay in racks that stretched to the ceiling and soft light mellowed the room in ambiance. Live jazz drifted over the clinking of glasses and the din of several conversations. When the waiter came to take their order, Damien said, "Manhattan. With a lemon. And a margarita for the lady. Patrón."

"I can't believe this place. I feel under-dressed here." Desiree said.

"Yeah, it's a nice place." He said, looking at the menu. "Have whatever you want. Don't give me that 'I'll just have salad' business either." He winked at her.

For most of the dinner he found himself more quiet than usual. He was taking her all in, listening to her talk in that way he would come to love, and when there was a lull in conversation he felt no urgency to continue it. He sat back and smiled, comfortable with the silence. His comfort made her comfortable. They ate well and drank lavishly and when the bill came he showed her the total which elicited a gasp from her, but Damien only smirked and said in his cool way,

"I got this."

His loft was only a few blocks away; they were holding hands as they walked towards it. Their talk became very animated and they laughed now and then. The streets were saturated with twilight and promise and when he squeezed her hand she squeezed it in return. When they reached his loft, he walked in and went to the cabinet above the stove. Pulling two glasses, he grabbed a bottle of wine and began to pour. She took a seat on the sofa, setting her small purse alongside her, admiring the furnishings and looking at the pictures he had displayed.

"This is a nice place. You definitely have good taste."

"Yeah, I'm proud of it," he said handing her a glass.

"You're well off."

"What do you mean?"

"Money is not really important to you, not how it is for most people."

He took a sip of his wine. "You think you have me all figured out, is that it?"

"Not quite. I'm just ... very intuitive."

"Well what have you intuited so far?"

"I'm not sure if I should say."

"Go on, tell me. I'm a big boy, I can take it."

She paused for a second and then spoke. "You don't feel you're as great as you project yourself to be. You chase things because you feel inadequate. But you're not. There's more to you than you let on, but it's not the things you think."

She had his attention now. "Go on."

"You flaunt things but you don't need to. And you're really a sweetheart. Deep down you believe in things. Like love. You're a romantic at heart."

Damien smirked. "I can assure you I'm quite the cynic."

"You say that, but I think underneath, there is something –I don't know, soft about you."

"Well I won't lie, there is a soft side of me, although not everyone sees it. I sense that there are parts of you that you don't reveal either. There's a wild side to you. There's a part of you that you haven't discovered yet."

"A wild side?"

"Pretty sure about it. You are full of surprises."

"I guess I'll have to keep that up then, surprising you."

"I'd like that. I need someone to keep me on my toes."

They talked for several hours in that fashion bordering intimacy. They held each other but not so close as to warrant commitment, for they both expressed a strong aversion to all things that caged them. Soft music was playing when they murmured to each other in the quiet dawn and they slept for two hours before rising and kissing each other good morning. He smiled when he walked her out, and closing the door, he took a deep breath. He looked out at the sun coming up over Detroit. He lit a cigar and reminisced about the past twelve hours.

That night was the exclamation point at the end of the sentence he had been forming in his mind; the sentence that was lost on other women: that failed to form with each new experience. In her, he saw contrasted the pride and grandeur he had grown comfortable with, and yet there was a quiet depth and a sadness that endeared her to him. In her company he felt more open, more pliable, and more sure of himself than ever. He went to sleep that morning content and satisfied with all things.

III.

For three glowing months that summer, the immediacy with which their lives intermeshed took on a serene and dreamlike quality. Days strung together in a felicitous fog and their personalities circled each other like binary stars. They found different sides to one another in which to lose themselves, and their shortcomings dulled in comparison to each new discovery. Life took on a new brightness and lucidity and in those shimmering moments, they gave not thought or precedence to those around them.

She charmed and dazzled him, and he in turn showed her a side of life that was fresh, dangerous and thrilling. She was drawn at first to the wild luster of his world; the high extravagance, the company he kept, and the places they frequented, but she soon became aware of a glaring flaw that he neither saw or acknowledged; that for all his confidence in himself and the places he was going, there was a restlessness and a hole that seemed bottomless. His insatiable appetite for sybaritic indulgences at first alarmed her, but she found that in spite of herself she was drawn to his untamed animalism and the passion and dominance that he exuded.

He introduced her in the following weeks to his close friends, to his family, and to the many acquaintances he knew. His friends loved her and even his father who was always sizing up anyone who came close to the family, said she was a "bright, sweet girl" with "a good head on her shoulders." He jokingly called her his daughter-in-law and kept inquiring about the date of the wedding, how many kids they wanted, and where they would honeymoon.

Summer continued on in a swelter, and when the heat broke on a weekend in late June, he took her to his family's private cabin a half hour north of the city. He had arranged it on an off weekend where they would be alone and not be disturbed by the many cousins and friends that enjoyed it in the summer months. It was a large extravagant house that had been in the family since the 1920s and the intense opulence of it left her again in speechless wonderment. Ornate wood paneling opened up to a great hall and there were spacious rooms, hidden nooks and she could tell that it was built for important prestigious people. The view looked out to Lake St. Clair, and there was a private beach that awaited them. They lunched in the main dining room and talked away a good hour. They napped, roused, then changed into swimwear and headed down to the water. After swimming and enjoying the day, they lay on the beach and he rolled them a joint. There was a calm that came over them. Her head found a comfortable place between his neck and his broad shoulder and when her warmth weighed on him, he took a whiff of her scent.

"You smell great." He said. "I could lie here all day." He inhaled and passed it to her.

"So could I." She took a long drag and was silent. She stared at the sky for a long while. "This doesn't feel real."

"What do you mean?"

"All of this. It just seems like a dream. I keep thinking I'm going to wake up from all of this at any moment." She turned her body towards him. "You just seem so much more on the edge of life than me."

"What can I say; you bring it out in me. You bring out a lot of things in me. Good things. What do I bring out in you?"

"A longing for some other life. One I've barely lived. One that's faster, more competitive, more daring. You make me feel like royalty."

"Princess Des."

"Queen Des."

That night they got drunk off of an aged red and talked late into the evening of all things. They walked along the beach, with the white gleam of the moon casting a shine upon them and the gentle lapping of the waves near their feet. She looked up at the stars.

"It's so strange to think that their light is coming to us from the past. The star might even be dead now. The universe is crazy. It makes me think about forever."

"I don't believe in forever," Damien said. "I believe in the present moment. Look at any clock and it's always right here, right now."

"I feel the same way. Always and forever are just words people use when they're too scared to face today." There was a pause. "Did you lose respect for me just now?"

"No," he smiled at her. "I gained it."

They revealed to each other the silent longings of their hearts and for a moment, it seemed like that first night they spent in the city. The air was pulsing with vibrant life and she looked more stunning than he had ever seen her. He pulled her into him, that night by the water, and their bodies melted into a quiet rhythm underneath the twinkling blanket of stars and the warm night breeze of summer.

IV.

The heat continued when they watched fireworks for three humid evenings in July. The parties were more frequent then, and it was often at Damien's loft where the weekend nights began and ended. It was three in the morning on one such night when the only people that remained were Desire, himself, two girls who were asleep, and a young artist named Dylan. He had come from Portland, to be a part of Detroit's "renaissance" as he called it. He spoke of it as a sort of mecca. He spoke of Motown in the 60s, the decline of the 70s, and the potential it held for artists of today. Though he was older by a few years, and was no doubt an intelligent man with few obvious flaws, Damien thought of him as a different and lesser breed. Dylan's tall slim figure was a contrast to the muscular toned bulk of himself and Damien viewed his idealism, his rosy view of the world, and the way he went about life, as unrealistic and frivolous.

"If you think you can save this city with art, you're mistaken. No amount of organic farming and graffiti will bring people back here," said Damien.

"What do you think the answer is then?" Dylan asked.

"You need investors. Big money guys. Movers and shakers. It's the businesses that are going to turn this city around."

"Well you aren't really doing anything to help the dilemma by partying in warehouses every weekend," said Dylan.

At this Damien got flustered. He wanted to fight the scrawny tattooed naive artist in front of him and he knew Dylan would be no match for him. But instead he took a sip of his drink and said, "I know some very wealthy people out here. My family runs in some very powerful circles. I want you to take a look outside my window. That's where the real change is going to come from. How much do you think is invested down there, in Midtown? How many millions?" Dylan was silent. "Do you even think in millions? Don't tell me how best to save this city." Damien cooled down. "Look, I don't mean to knock what you do, you just don't know the real truth of things. But I just wanna have a good time tonight." Damien shook Dylan's hand with his powerful grip and patted him on the back. "Another vodka?" Dylan nodded yes.

It was not long after this that the conversation turned to art. At this, Desiree lit up and shifted herself from the bored nonchalance of the previous debate, to a more vibrant enthused demeanor. She inquired about Dylan's taste in art.

"Van Gogh would probably be my favorite," said Dylan.

"I love Van Gogh! Starry Night is my favorite by him. That and The Night Cafe. How long have you been painting?" Desiree could hardly control her enthusiasm.

"Since I was very young. Four or five maybe. Do you paint?"

"Yeah, I'm majoring in graphic design but I'm really a painter at heart. Do you work with oils? Acrylics?

"Oils. I like acrylic but it dries too fast, and it doesn't last as long either."

"I wish I could afford oils, but they are too expensive. I need to get new brushes too. I work with acrylics." Desiree looked down at the floor. "I wish I painted more."

"Come by my studio sometime and I will show you some techniques."

"Oh, I would love that! But I don't want to burden you. You must be very busy."

"Not at all, it would be my pleasure. Do you work with knives? Brushes?

"Both. More so with brushes."

"I only use knives. I find the knife lends itself to more dramatic approaches. It is more aggressive, more bold than a brush. I will show you sometime. Next week?"

"Next week sounds lovely."

Damien heard more and more about Dylan in the following weeks. "His style is so expressive. He's so passionate." Desiree would say. She met him several times at his studio when the seasons began to change, but the exact nature of these visits and to what extent Dylan was more attuned to the finer rhythms of her began to gnaw at Damien although he remained smug as always.

Her visits with Dylan became more frequent, but she always assured Damien of their innocence.

When Desiree's classes resumed in the fall he saw less and less of her. She was busy with school and he was busy with his stocks and his real estate properties, but he hated hearing about Dylan just as Desiree hated to hear Damien talk of volatility, position sizes and hedging the market.

Summer began to wind down and it was on a cool Saturday when they were weighing their options for the coming evening.

"There's nothing happening tonight. There's the DIA. There's Greektown, Motor City... "

"I want you to come to Dylan's. You should see his work; I think you would like it."

"Another night. But you go. Have fun, have a good story to tell me later."

Desiree did not come home from Dylan's that night, and when he called her the next day she did not answer. When he saw her next –four days later– she was quieter, and he sensed that something was amiss. They gave one word answers to each other's questions, and they could not look each other in the eye for very long. It was then that she told him;

"I need a break. I can't be with you right now, Damien. I just can't."

"No. You can't," Damien said trying to control himself. "I can't be with someone who's not on the same level as me."

"What? How can you say that?"

"Just go Des. Just leave. "

Several months passed, and for a time, he attempted to block her out of his life completely. He threw himself into his work, his stocks, his family and friends. He was constantly busy, and when there were matters which did not make him money, he was throwing parties or attending them. Months turned into years and for a long while everything about her remained fresh and vivid to him as if she had left him only yesterday, but soon he found himself thinking of her less and less. She began to dim in his mind but when she did he became all the more sentimental and passionate. "Des" he would say, looking out at the skyline. He would shake his head and bite his lips. When his friends would ask him what was on his mind during the moments when he would grow silent, he would reduce her to a single word; "her." They did not raise the question again. He took to drink, to distractions and filled his life with new women; who quite often seemed dull and forgettable. But no woman, however clever and attractive she was, could quite fill the void that he had created for himself; for all other women paled in comparison to the grand ideal that he had fostered of her in his mind.

But this was not the Desiree who had walked with him on the midnight beach during that hot summer. This was the Desiree he had created and magnified through the years in fragmented reveries. This Desiree took on a more mythic and voluptuous form than the one he had known in the flesh. Even though they no longer remained in contact, she stayed murderously close to his heart, revolving in his orbit like a great invincible star on which he dreamed and navigated the trajectory of his life.

The nights that he found his bed empty, he would lie awake and ponder the ways in which he was inferior in Desiree's eyes. He tormented himself with the known and unknown in the dark of his loft. He tried to determine what it was about Dylan that she was drawn to, what he possessed that he could not give her. He felt more and more as time went on, that the chance for salvaging what remained of them was slipping from him, perhaps forever. He had heard friends tell him to give it up. "Sometimes, it takes more strength to let things go than it does to pursue them," they would tell him. When they did, he would say, "I know." and look off into space, expecting the silence to be sufficient motive to change the subject. He let them change it. To give up now meant to surrender; and never in his life had he surrendered, especially not something as precious as her.

Spring slipped into summer with a leisurely heat that revitalized him, and he felt his life beginning to bloom again. The city had breathed its first full breath of life, and his face was flush with enthusiastic hedonism when he looked out at the city. "These streets belong to me. This city and everything in it," he thought as he buttoned his shirt. "Summer is mine."

An hour later Damien was in the casino where he lost close to a grand on three consecutive losing hands of blackjack before making it up on the fourth and fifth. He left and worked his way through the bars to a street fair he had heard advertised. He met up with friends and dropped acid on a whim. An hour passed and then another. As he walked through the throng of people, the faces began to blend into one another. The crowd throbbed and groaned with revelry, and in his drunkenness the sounds of music and laughter swirled into a hedonistic cacophony. He became disoriented, and visions slipped past as if in a dream. And then, through the crowd he glimpsed familiar distortions of flesh; eyes and hair and lips. Damien looked again, but she was lost in the shifting of the lively mix. He called out her name, and tried to muscle his way through the crowd. He called out to her again and went to where she was walking. He turned a corner into an alley. There were a few people lining the walls, drinking and smoking.

"You look lost." Damien heard someone say. "Are you lost?" they said again. Then riotous laughter as he staggered back out into the street.

"Hey come back here!" He heard, but he paid no attention.

He thought he saw her again, and when he came up and said her name, she turned to him, but it was not her. Her face was too old, her eyes the wrong color. She gave him a disgusted look and he walked away, still in hopeless pursuit. The feverish din of the crowd turned now into a maddening howl as he quickened his pace. The faces became grotesque forms, caricatures of people he had known and yet they remained unrecognizable.

His mind became soft and dark, and after an uncertain amount of time, he found himself in a loud venue, the lights flashing in pulses on cavorting bodies that gleamed with a light sheen of sweat. His movements felt loose and rigid, and he soon found himself in the company of a slender woman with dark stunning features. The music pulsed in his head and he quickly forgot her name after she had said it. They danced and drew closer. In a subtle corner they were not subtle and they explored each other freely.

"Let's get out of here" he said. "This place was dead an hour ago and there's no use waiting around."

She said something that he did not hear, and he said again as he began walking "Des, let's get out of here." He turned to find her, but she was gone.

"Des. Des... "

Time passed.

"... you alright?" An unknown voice asked.

"I'm fine."

Lights, music, faces, movement, and then darkness. He awoke in his bed still in his clothes. His heart and head pulsed. He stayed in bed that day and did not answer the phone when it rang.

Three months whirled past and it was on a Friday that he found himself exhausted. That night was the first night in months that he had been alone, not of his own accord. He refused to let loneliness take hold, and headed off to a dive a few blocks from his loft. The place was dead, save for a few unfamiliar faces. He ordered a double. The bottles against the lighted glass resembled the skyline if he was looking at sunset but looking at himself in the mirrored wall of the bar made him feel all the more isolated and embarrassed. He finished it quickly and left.

While he was walking back, he found himself being struck by sudden sentimentalities which at first he attributed to the whiskey, but upon further meditation, realized that they were in fact feelings which he had buried in hopes that they would be forgotten and dismissed. He thought again of that evening in the city. The blur of the lights remained fresh and alive as if he had seen them only the night before. It was then that he thought to call Desiree. After a half an hour of telling himself all the reasons not to, he at last gave in and waited anxiously as the phone rang. Having not talked with her in so long, he wondered what her reaction would be.

"Hello."

"Hey. It's Damien."

"Oh," she said after a startled pause. "Oh hey."

Their conversation continued in a light manner for the better part of an hour. They enjoyed catching up and reminiscing, and yet there was a faint tension that lingered in their voices. Their speech took on a quicker and brighter rhythm, as if they were both building up to some long awaited moment, some unforeseeable unidentifiable crescendo. Words and phrases slipped off the tip of one tongue and the reply to them on the others. The realization of what was both on their minds came closest to its fruition when Desiree brought up the time they were first alone with each other in the city.

"I barely remember that night. I mean I do, but only certain things."

"I remember it well. You were wearing that top, the black one. And you had your hair up the way I like it."

"Wow you do have quite the memory."

"Who could ever forget a night like that?" There was a slight pause and then, "You know sometimes, I... Well, never mind."

"No go on. What were you going to say?"

"It's not important. I'll tell you some other time."

"Tell me," she said.

"Don't worry about it, it's nothing. Besides, it's nearly dawn. The sun's coming up, and you should get your sleep."

"Alright, well I will hold you to that. But you're right, it's getting late. I think I'd better go."

"Yeah me too." Again another pause, this one longer than the first, as if they were both waiting for the other to start. Finally he said,

"It was nice talking with you."

"Yeah, it was. I'm glad you called."

"Goodnight Desiree."

"Goodnight Damien."

V.

For many years they did not talk, and whenever he saw her friends in the city, he would chat briefly with them, inquiring about her. He learned that she had studied abroad for a year, and then moved to Portland for a little while before relocating to Chicago. As more of her friends got married or moved out of state he gradually lost track of her but his conviction never wavered. "She will come around," he told himself. "When circumstances are more favorable, she will come around."

After a while, he fell into a depression, and his life began to falter. His dejection and listlessness soon became apparent to those around him, and they urged him to take a break from everything. "You're pushing yourself too hard. You need to slow down," they would tell him. He was overworked, but of all the phrases they uttered to him, that phrase was the most hated and most foreign to him. Never in his whole life had he taken anything slow. There was no time for that. "If you are not moving forwards you are moving backwards," he would tell himself, and to get ahead one needed to move faster. The mediocrity of their lives, and the contented ways in which they lived were alien to him, for he despised their lack of ambition, and he in all his life had never been content save for those twelve weeks during that hot summer. He wondered then if this was the best it would be for him, and if he was not made to be content as some are made to be mediocre or made to be excellent. The whole thing left him miserable and bitter. He decided not to dwell on it, but as the old restlessness came back to him, and as a way to appease those concerned for him, he decided at last to finally assent to their suggestions.

This in turn led him on a three month excursion to Europe, where he drank himself into a deeper depression during the first month, while he was staying in Paris. He was on the other side of the world, but he felt immensely close to home and to her and yet immensely distant. He thought of the things he knew about her and the mysteries he had not penetrated. She had always been elusive, and he tried to think about the things that made her smile. It had been seven years since he had seen Desiree, and three since he had talked with her last. Frequently he thought of her. "She would love it here," he found himself saying. "She would absolutely love it here."

Damien coasted on in a daze until his stay came to an end on a foreign beach. He was in a stupor watching the sunset and felt everything slipping from him. He felt as if he had lost a season out of his life, some elusive summer just out of his reach. What felt worse was the feeling that he had squandered every other season in search of the lost one.

He picked himself up and went back to his hotel. He lit a cigarette on the patio, finished it and collapsed on the bed. The phone rang and on the line he heard a familiar voice. It was an old friend from the neighborhood; he told him that Desire had tried to contact him, but he would not reveal any further details. Whether out of lack of knowledge or some ulterior motive, Damien couldn't be sure. He booked a flight that night and in two days he was headed back to The States, his nerves on fire, his heart and mind alive with rapid emotions.

When he finally contacted her, her voice seemed different but he could not put his finger on it. The life that so emanated from it seemed diminished in some way. His mind was filled with many things, but he remained cool and kept their conversation brief.

They agreed to meet for lunch in two days. The forty eight hours that passed since their phone conversation seemed to him an eternity, and though he tried not to show it, he felt nervous and on edge. He got a haircut, shaved and bought a new shirt for the occasion. He arrived a few minutes early and waited in anticipation for her, trying to clear his head though it was buzzing with excitement and unanswered questions. He wondered if she had changed much since he last saw her. The thought frightened him, but what frightened him more was the change he felt himself on the brink of.

When she finally arrived, he almost didn't recognize her. Her hair was shorter and lighter. She looked thinner and more frail. She looked distressed. She still carried herself in that confident manner that first attracted him, but there was something new and strange in her gait. They greeted each other with a long hug and he kissed her on the cheek.

"Wow, you look great. Jesus, it's been so long, but you really look great."

"Thanks."

They took their seats across from each other and after the waitress came to take their orders, they both relaxed a little. It was not long until their dialogue took on a serious tone, and she finally revealed the nature of their meeting.

"I have to tell you something." she said.

"Anything, Des. You can tell me anything."

She looked away and was quiet for a long time. And then she said words that seemed to shake Damien out of the room.

"I'm sick." Her voice cracked and she said, "I'm not going to get better. The doctors say I'm looking at three months."

He remained speechless for a second, and then he grabbed her hand .

"Jesus Christ." His breath quickened, "Jesus Des. I'm sorry. I don't know what to say. When did this happen?"

"It came on pretty suddenly. Sometimes if they catch it in time... "

Her voice cracked again and she couldn't say any more. He squeezed her hand harder. Then he got up and hugged her. They embraced each other for a long while, not knowing what to say, not wanting the tears to come, but they did.

The funeral came a month after their reunion at the cafe. He could not bear to stay long. For three months he could not think straight and he remained very aloof and withdrawn. A song remained in his head, one that so moved him upon hearing it he had to pull over to sob when he heard it alone in his car. He found himself humming it when no one was around.

... For they could not love you, but still your love was true...
... This world was never meant for one as beautiful as you...

He turned thirty seven months after Desiree's passing. He smiled now and was more cordial and his friends and family said it was great to have him back. He had been sober for six months and was training to run a marathon. So carefully did he conceal his anguish, that those around him confused his escape into his work as nothing more than the inexorable vigor with which he pursued all of his affairs. But this was not the life he had envisioned for himself and some part of him still ached. He was tired, but he feared that if he didn't stay occupied, he might turn from morose to hopeless. There was a pink band that replaced the large face of an expensive watch he wore on his wrist, and he tugged at it now and then when he was alone.

It was in one of those sullen moods he had come to know that he thought of Dylan. He had not seen him at the funeral and he had not spoken to him in years. He decided to look him up and to make amends. It would give him closure at least.

In a week's time he was sitting in Dylan's studio in Portland. He didn't know what to expect. He said he just wanted to talk things over. Dylan greeted him at the door, and Damien could smell liquor on his breath when he said,

"Damien Roth. Long time no see eh? You haven't changed a bit. Come in." Damien sat down at the table and looked around at the studio. Empty bottles and sensual abstract portraits of women were lying around. Several of them resembled Desiree, but he couldn't be sure.

"Drink?" Dylan said, pouring a vodka.

"I don't drink anymore."

"Look at you. Damien Roth, clean as a whistle now. Who would have thought?" He finished his drink in one gulp and poured another one. "I would have never seen that coming. People don't change."

"Some people don't change, you're right. But Des... She was always changing. Too fast for us to notice. She always said she was trying to keep up with me, with my lifestyle and my indulgences. You know how I am. But I'll tell you, it was I who was trying to keep up with her. She... Well Christ, I don't have to tell you. You of all people should know. She was something else, that woman. Something else entirely."

Dylan did not move from his seat and his expression or stare did not change. A long moment passed and then he said, "You ruined her."

"What?"

"You ruined her. Corrupted her. You put things in her head and she tried to live up to them. Said she never felt right with you, never felt good enough. All those parties, all that money, that lifestyle... Always said you were too good for her. She was a virgin before she met you, did you know that?   But she never got over you. She said she never loved anyone like she loved you. You ruined that poor girl Damien. You ruined every beautiful thing about her. "

"You're drunk; you don't know what you're talking about."

Dylan rose from his chair. "She was never the same after you. Never could give her heart to anyone after that. She destroyed herself."

Damien was in shock, and all he could say was "No, no... "Damien felt something deep inside of him coming to the surface and he turned to leave.

"You killed her!" Dylan screamed before lunging at Damien. Damien fell to the floor and they wrestled on the ground before Dylan hit him over the head with a lamp that had fallen down during the scuffle. Damien lay stunned and bleeding as Dylan choked him more.

"Listen to yourself. Please," Damien managed to gasp as Dylan pressed both hands with full might against his Adams apple. Damien struggled and let out another faint "please... "

And it was in that moment that he saw Damien the most vulnerable he had ever seen him. In that moment he looked Damien dead in the eye and those cold dominating eyes looked back at him and revealed with a sincere humility, not terror or malice, but a pleading and a longing. Dylan's hand increased the pressure on Damien's throat and in the last seconds before the life escaped his gaze, Dylan realized the full gravity and weight of that look. Damien was mocking him in his last glare; mocking him because it was he who was the better man in the end, he who would be reunited with her first, and it was a pleading for Dylan to get it over with sooner, for last longing in his eyes was not for death or life, but for her.

14.
It's Raining Again
A. J. Huffman

for what seems like the 41st consecutive night.
My body is aching, the ground is sinking,
and animals are beginning to huddle in pairs.
There is a rumor circulating about
some old guy on the beach piecing
together an oversized yacht from scrap
metal and drift wood.   I went down to fill out
my application for the inaugural cruise, discovered
that having a split personality does not qualify
me as being a pair.   Instead, he sold me an umbrella
and two planks in the form of a cross.

15.
Jamie
Heather Moser

Her mind was made up. She needed to grow and explore. As she sat in her driveway with her car packed and the key in the ignition, she knew it was time to leave. She had waited around far too long for a change of heart in her lover, but he was too stubborn to listen to her pleas for alteration of his attitude and behavior. So, with a small sense of hesitancy, she turned the key and pulled out of the driveway, heading as far away as she could possibly go.

She rolled the windows down and turned on the fan. Her A/C was broken, it had been for years, but other expenses always seemed to be more pressing. She wasn't allowed to drive often anyway and certainly not for any distance, so he said it wasn't important. It was an early July morning; almost five years to the day that she had first moved to this town with him, and away from her friends and family. He promised that his love would fill the gaps in her soul that were a result of being ripped away from her home. That was a promise he ultimately could not fulfill. It had been little more than words. He had always been a man of words with an unbelievable lack of ability to follow through. Eventually, the only rationalization that made any sense to her was that he never had the intent to follow through; he was just trying to appease her in an attempt to make her stay. The only action he knew how to take was to throw her to the floor in a fit of rage if she was brave or fed up enough to question him.

Although the sun had just started to elucidate the sky, the heat was nearly unbearable, just as it had been the day they moved in together. The five years that followed were filled with every range of emotion imaginable. They had moments of pure ecstasy and hope, but those memories were darkened by the shadow of the endless amounts of fighting and arguing. Tears ran like rivers from both of them on a weekly basis. They had never really been meant for each other, but they were young and naïve. Part of the reason they had even made the decision to move away together was an attempt to prove all of their doubters wrong. Everyone from friends to family never thought it would work, and they were determined to show them otherwise. How foolish it all seemed now.

Stubbornness is a wonderful quality but only when applied in the proper circumstances. That was a lesson she had learned from this wreck of a relationship. She would also consider listening to her family and friends a little more next time. How could she have ever thought that every single person in her life was out to make her miserable? How could she have allowed him to manipulate her into isolation? Never again, she told herself. That would be the last man to make her feel worthless.

After a few miles of silence, she turned on her carefully planned playlist. Mumford and Sons blared through her speakers and the rows of trees that lined the roads flew by her window as she sped out of her small town and down some unknown roads that were bound to take her anywhere but here... to any place but her past life, and to any future lover other than the man who had failed her miserably for nearly a fifth of her lifetime. She needed a better life, and she was taking the reins. She had taken the most difficult step by leaving, but she was now heading to a safer place.

Jamie drove for hours, exhausting her playlist many times through. She eventually had to resort to the radio, endlessly searching through channels with which she was unfamiliar to find a song fitting her mood. She lost count of the number of times a song was drowned out by static before it finished. After the sun made its journey across the sky and fell below the horizon, she began to feel a little fatigued. With a gas tank nearing empty, she needed to stop for gas anyway. Sleep was beginning to weigh heavily on her mind. Unfortunately for her, she had managed to come upon a stretch of highway that seemed to have no exits in sight. As the night progressed, it became suspicious that she hadn't passed any cars in quite some time. Just as her mind began to wonder as to the possible reasons for a lack of traffic, she passed a green sign illuminated by her headlights:

Exit 29 3 miles

She didn't remember what highway she had taken all those hours ago, but she was eager to take a rest, regardless of where she was. About a half mile before the exit, rain started to drizzle just enough to warrant use of her windshield wipers. Odd, she thought. The weather report had called for clear skies in the neighboring states for at least another two days, and she was doubtful she could have made it that far already. Reluctantly, she rolled up her windows to save the luggage that took up most of the seating in her car. Hopefully she would find an inn soon, the constant breeze that had been coming in her windows was the only thing keeping her from falling asleep for the last seventy miles, and now it was gone.

Finally the exit sign shined brightly ahead, and Jamie put on her turn signal. She slowly merged into the right hand lane and came to a stop sign at the end of the off ramp. Another green sign was there for travelers, showing only two arrows, both pointing to the right. One was for a gas station only two miles away and the other for an inn just a mile beyond that. How convenient, she thought, after miles of nothing, everything I need is in one place. It must be fate! She turned right on to a small two-lane road that looked as if it hadn't been touched by the department of transportation in years. Potholes and cracked pavement made the next couple of miles a much rougher ride than she had anticipated.

As she headed down the dark road, she saw her first destination ahead. The gas station emanated a pale blue glow amidst an otherwise pitch-black roadway. She put on her left turn signal and eased into the gas station, pulling up to one of the many available pumps. After turning off the car, Jamie stepped out of the vehicle and headed around to the pumps, pulling her bankcard out of her purse as she walked. She looked at the pump in disbelief. No place for a card. A sign had been taped haphazardly near the nozzle that read "Cash Only-Pay Inside." A bit frustrated, she shoved her card back into her wallet and quickly turned toward the station, keeping her head down and sighing to herself while the rain began to pour down with more ferocity than before. She didn't have cash. Hopefully there would at least be an ATM inside; otherwise, her journey may end here tonight. She would be forced to beg for a job as a gas station attendant until she earned enough money to pay for a full tank.

Pulling the door open, Jamie stepped inside, wiping the water off of her forehead. When the moisture left her eyes and they began to focus, she looked around until she saw a cashier down an aisle to the right. The register was right beside the windows, most certainly allowing him to witness her walk sulkily from her car to the door.

"Long night?" inquired the extremely thin and rough looking middle-aged man with salt and pepper scruff as he peered over the top of his oversized glasses.

He had a half smile, but Jamie could not decide whether the smile was a result of amusement at her obvious frustration or an odd greeting that didn't feel at all welcoming. It was extremely off-putting, but she was trying her best to not be persuaded to feel a certain way based on the man's appearance alone.

"Actually, yes. It has been a long day and even longer night. I need to fill my gas tank and head to the inn down the road for a little rest before I continue my journey."

Through her exhaustion, she tried to return his smile as she came up to the register. She placed her soaking purse on the counter without thinking. The rainwater that had saturated her canvas bag began to rapidly rush out. The remaining stack of the newspapers sitting beside the register quickly became damp as it soaked up the rain like a wick. Adding embarrassment to her palate of emotions, she removed her bag from the counter and somehow managed a smile. In place of his smile, however, was now a face of disgust as he looked at his damaged goods. His dark eyes flicked up to meet hers as he aggressively ripped the stack of papers off of the counter and dropped them into a trashcan that was out of her line of vision. It was clear he was not pleased she had come into the store now.

"How much do you need? Forty?" He replied in a rather cold manner.

"Actually, I don't have any cash. I don't know what to do."

"We take cash only." He retorted with a snarl.

"I don't have any, but I need gas. Isn't there something we can do? Do you have an ATM around anywhere?" She was beginning to feel desperate and overly anxious to leave.

"Oh, I see. You are one of *those* people. Too important to touch money, so you just carry around plastic for convenience. You think it's dirty don't you? You probably don't even remember what a dollar bill or coin feels like, do you? Listen, you may be the norm where you come from, but we work hard around here and aren't too good to actually hold the money we have earned."

Her desperation was now turning to anger and bitterness. Who was this man to throw out such harsh accusations against her?

He didn't know her at all. She would not tolerate any man to belittle her, stranger or not.

"Just answer my question. Do you have an ATM somewhere in this shack you so proudly call a gas station or not? If not, where is the nearest one? I will walk if I have to at this point!"

"Well, so quick to anger. For such an outspoken woman, one would think she would be more aware of her surroundings. It is by the front door. You walked right by it in your hurry to damage my papers. Twenty-five dollars' worth of papers, by the way. Be sure to take that out extra, because you have cost me at least that from your thoughtlessness tonight."

"Are you kidding me?! Those papers were from yesterday! No one in their right mind would by a day's old newspaper. You would have thrown them away anyway. Don't use me as an excuse for a quick buck. It isn't going to happen."

She stomped back toward the front of the store to the oldest ATM machine she had ever seen. Despite its obvious age, it didn't appear that it had ever been used. The buttons had no sign of wear. In fact, the layer of dust all over it told a story of either a machine that had rarely seen use or employees who never cleaned the store at all. Looking around and seeing that everything else was virtually spotless, she concluded that, just as the clerk had so boldly insinuated, no one around here used the ATM. The chain that owned the station probably required the machine, but the lack of care for its appearance showed obvious disdain for its presence by the locals.

She inserted her card, entered her pin number, and waited what seemed like an eternity to punch in the amount she wanted to take out. She decided two hundred dollars would be safe. Enough for gas and hotel room, assuming that the inn just down the road would have the same backwards stance as this attendant. Better to be safe than sorry, at any rate. She didn't want to deal with any more judgments from strangers today.

Heading back to the counter, she slammed down two twenties on the counter, making sure to hold eye contact with the man who had managed to piss her off in only a matter of minutes.

"I'm at pump two. Thanks."

She stomped toward the front of the store, throwing the door open as she exited the building. Once outside, she began filling her tank, her back to the windows and the cashier. She felt like someone was watching her. She discreetly used her shoulder to wipe the rain off the side of her face. While shrugging, she looked back toward the man who was indeed peering out of the window, watching her every move as he talked on a phone. He was smiling, however. It was a very unsettling smile. She wondered whom he could be calling so late at night. Hopefully not the police under some stupid pretense of disorderly conduct, she thought to herself. The pump clicked once it hit the forty dollar mark, she placed the nozzle back on the pump, and closed her gas tank. As she walked around the backside of her car to get to the driver's door, she boldly looked at the man as he was hanging up the receiver. He gave her a huge smile, revealing his yellowed rotting teeth, and waved. Chills went up her spine, and she rushed into the car to speed out of the parking lot, tearing down the road toward the nameless inn.

It wasn't more than a few seconds before she saw the inn, sitting on a corner of a four way stop. In between the swipes of her windshield wipers, she could see a dark wooden sign with fading white letters, illuminated by a pale yellow spotlight:

Crossroads Inn

Finally, a place to rest for a while. She felt a wave of relief as she turned into the gravel parking lot of the ill-lit inn. She negotiated several potholes before parking at the only door that could even remotely be considered an entrance. The whole setup of the inn was a bit confusing to her, because she couldn't see any rooms. The place looked like a huge log cabin, aged and beginning to look a bit dilapidated with what appeared to be candlelight shining through at least a dozen of its dingy windows. From the outside it looked like the Crossroads Inn was a fire hazard that needed to be condemned long ago.

That must not have been the consensus of the locals, however, as she could hear the merrymaking inside even though, curiously enough, there was an absence of vehicles in the parking lot. Maybe there is additional parking in the back, she thought. The front door was much heavier than it looked, with a huge vertical handle that she could barely fit her hands around. She had to grab the handle with both hands and use all of her body weight to get it to budge even a little. Why this old fashioned door that looked like it came straight out of a medieval castle was used for an entrance was beyond her understanding. It creaked too, ever so loudly. Her hope of slipping in relatively unnoticed was squashed when the hinges started screeching and grinding like they were about to give in and cause the massive door to fall to the floor. She shuddered at the sound.

A room full of men and women witnessed her entrance, each of them stopping their jovial conversations to stare at her in silence. She was so taken aback by the scene that was happening before her. First of all, she was not exactly expecting to walk into a bar. She saw no check-in desk. Sure, she had been in a handful of hotels over the years that had bars, but they were always in another area of the hotel, or, at the very least, away from the entrance. Never had she just walked into a bar before finding a place to check in. She began to wonder if perhaps she had missed a different door that was for the actual inn and not the tavern. For a moment she felt a bit of embarrassment for not recalling that the term 'inn' can mean an establishment for drinking. Suddenly she began to panic at the thought that perhaps this inn didn't even have any beds, but the building was so large that there had to be more to it than a bar. Regardless, it wouldn't hurt to have a drink after the interaction she had had just down the road at the gas station.

The scenery of the room was breathtaking. Everything was wooden. It was rustic and inviting. The mugs that were in the hands of the hushed crowd before her were even made of wood. The people, though, appeared to not be overly enthused that Jamie had just entered the room. They made the room cold. Not a smile, not a sound, not a movement. It was as if she was from another planet, some sort of being they had never seen before, or worse, some being they knew and disdained. She did not feel welcomed at all, and she was a tiny bit scared.

One man in particular made her skin crawl. He was the only one in the room who was not staring at her or remaining motionless. Instead his fingers slowly circled around the rim of his mug in a predatory fashion while staring at the floor. At least she was assuming he was staring at the floor, his head was bowed with a hood covering his hair, casting its shadow over his eyes and rendering her unable to truly decipher where his gaze was set. The man sitting next to him appeared to have had a bit too much to drink, as he was passed out in his chair, slumped over while leaning against the wall. Drunkards didn't bother her, especially if they were already passed out for the night; but, the other man was no drunkard.

After a few minutes, the brooding man in the corner broke the silence of the room as he slowly stood up from his table. His chair screeched. The back of his legs pushed it away from him as they stretched to their full length. He was much taller than he had appeared. Once he stood, the entire room looked back at him in a sudden in sync motion. Everyone gasped and fell silent just as quickly. She couldn't help but feel she had stirred some sort of monster that the locals weren't even aware had been lurking in the back corner of the bar amongst the shadows. Whatever he was, his very appearance made them look just as uneasy as she felt.

Jamie's blood began to run cold. He took a step to the side in order to circumvent the table before he slowly pushed his hood back behind his head, revealing silvery eyes that seemed to glow as they reflected the fires from the candles that were flickering all throughout the room. His face was encompassed in darkness with both the hair on his head and his beard appearing to be as black as the outfit he was wearing. His steel gaze met hers and, in that instant, the room seemed to gain a sense of levity. The patrons resumed their normal business, just as if they sensed with much relief that this was purely a matter between the silver-eyed man and the terrified girl. By the time he made his way to Jamie, who was still standing frozen near the absurdly heavy front door, she felt like she had become invisible to everyone but this strange man.

"Ah, Jamie. So you have returned despite our last several conversations? I must say that I am highly disappointed in you. Momus called just a short time ago to let me know you had already spoken to him—in quite a different and aggressive tone than normal, I might add--and to alert me that you were on your way here. I came immediately to talk to you one last time."

He was standing directly in front of her now, extending his hand to her in a rather non-threatening manner. Involuntarily she took his outstretched hand, which was freezing cold, and her entire body shivered. She could have sworn the temperature dropped several degrees as he approached and now she could physically feel the reason why.

"Momus? Who is Momus?" She screamed in her thoughts. "Who is this? Why am I now walking with him back to his table? Why do I feel so helpless right now? What in the world is going on? What am I doing here? Why can't I speak out loud?"

"Slow down, we have all the time you need to talk. This is going to be the most important conversation you have ever had in your life, so, please, take your time. Absorb all that I am about to tell you. Momus is an associate of mine. You will have to forgive his abrasive attitude. He tends to get a little touchy at times; although, I find that aspect of his personality rather endearing. You are no longer completely in control of your body because you are not exactly in your body. Your job right now is to listen as closely as possible."

She had to completely resign herself to the idea that she would not have any control. He had just read her thoughts without her saying a word aloud, and he responded without vocalizing at all. None of this seemed rational, yet it didn't feel as if she would have much say in how the rest of this interaction would unfold. She decided to give in to the moment, pushing her fear into the back of her mind and allowing her curiosity to come forth to be satisfied. Having reached this conclusion, she realized they were already at the table. He pulled a chair out for her, putting her diagonally across from the man still sleeping against the wall. He sat down directly across from her. The rest of the evening's conversation would have appeared, to an outsider, to consist of merely exchanged glances and nothing more. They spoke through thought only, their dialogue private, the only hints of emotion coming from her eyes as the night progressed.

He continued, "We have met before. Actually, I am uncomfortable with how well we know one another. It is not my duty to become so concerned with human affairs, but for some reason you keep appearing on my list. Quite frankly, I am getting annoyed with you, but I feel mild relief in knowing that this could potentially be my final meeting with you for quite some time."

She was unable to form any thought.

He resumed, "Let me start over. You are on the edge of death. You are at the crossroads of purgatory and everyone you see here is enjoying what little they can in this place. They can only interact with one another, but they cannot interact with anyone outside of purgatory. They will be here for as long as they need until they find a way to pass on to the next cycle of being. Some will never leave because they can't find rest or they simply refuse. Regardless of their reasoning, they still crave interaction, which is what you see manifesting before you this evening. You, Jamie, are not ready for purgatory yet; although, you do prefer to flirt with the veil a great deal."

"What do you mean flirt with the veil? I don't want to be here!"

"I beg to differ. Your behavior tells a different story. This is not your first visit to the Crossroads Inn. Each time, the patrons give you the same reaction. They are cold and quiet, in awe that after having been given so many chances, you still choose to come back here. Many of them were not given the luxury you have been given. They can see you, but they cannot speak to you. You look different to them, because there is a faint life force about you that causes you to appear shade-like. To them: you, my dear, are the ghost of what each of them once had, and they recognize you still have hope."

"Fine, they recognize me; but why did they appear to be surprised at your presence?"

"Ha! Well, that is simple. They were in the middle of a wonderful time... something that is a rare enough occurrence here. I am the reaper of souls who moves beings between realms, often to a less desired destination. My name is Thanatos, and my presence could have signaled a very different end for everyone's night. Once they saw that my business was with you, however, they relaxed. You have to enjoy the present, you know. I can appear in the blink of an eye."

"You are Death?"

"If you wish to call me by that name, yes. I prefer my given name, though; it tends to let people listen to me a bit longer before going into total shock at the realization of who is standing before them."

"I am not sure I feel more at ease with that knowledge." She turned her head to the side, shaking it in disbelief. Her gaze left his to look down at the wooden table. She looked around the room at the people who now seemed to have a hazy look around their bodies; their movements appearing to leave vapor trails behind them. She stared at them for a while. They were hauntingly beautiful. Finally, she turned back to Thanatos. "But, you said you know me well. I don't remember you or this inn."

"Yes, that is part of the problem. Perhaps if you had remembered our interactions we wouldn't be talking right now. My threats should have been enough to cause you to change your behavior, but apparently the situation has not gotten grave enough yet. It will soon though, and the next time I see you, there will be no communication between us; you will only follow me."

"Change my behavior? What do you mean? I did change my behavior. I am trying to start a new life. That is what led me here... I think. I headed out for a new life this morning. Although now I have no idea how I ended up here tonight."

"No, your journey here was not what actually happened. The first half of the day, you thought you were recalling, was your subconscious living out what it knows will save you. The minute you saw rain, your subconscious gave way and your soul took over the wheel as you started to enter purgatory."

"I didn't leave him yet? But I am sick of the abuse. The physical is bad enough, but the emotional is far worse."

"This time the physical abuse will be far worse. He has read your journal in which you fantasized about leaving him. He has decided that you can't have even an illusion of being able to leave. While you are sleeping in your realm, he is growing full of rage at what he has seen in your writings. He is unable to let go of his anger once he gets fixated on it, Jamie. You know this. This is why we have spoken before; each time right before he has violently lashed out at you. Next time, and there will be a next time, you will not survive it. Jamie, I am telling you now, when you wake up, run. Go. You must leave before he knows you are awake. Live out the fantasy for which your subconscious is yearning. It is the only way you will survive. I cannot reiterate enough, Jamie: you will die if you don't change your behavior and leave. You cannot change him."

Her head was swimming. How had she not remembered these interactions? More importantly, how did she become the battered woman? What did she do to deserve this? Oh, none of that mattered now. She needed to find a way to remember this when she awoke.

"How can I remember the warning this time if I never have before?" She thought with desperation, looking at Thanatos through her tear filled eyes.

"Well, that is why I decided this was beyond my powers this time. Granted, I can usually strike fear into the rare cases, like yours, that I am assigned, and I hate failing any task, even if I don't particularly care for them in the first place." Thanatos kicked the chair of the sleeping man, rousing him from his slumber. This man looked almost completely opposite of Thanatos, with long dirty blonde hair. The only similarities resided in his large stature that was evident even as he had remained slumped in his chair. He also had those same eerie silver eyes.

"A drunkard? You felt a drunkard would somehow help me?"

The blonde man leaned forward in a flash, getting within a few inches of Jamie's face. For the first time since she entered the Crossroads Inn, someone spoke out loud, and he did so with searing anger, "Surely you aren't talking about me, lost soul. I am far more powerful than you think, and I am no drunkard!"

That was the last vocalization of the night, as Thanatos pushed his thoughts through the wall of ire that was firmly placed in Hypnos' mind. "Calm down, brother. The girl is overwhelmed right now. You are doing this favor for me, anyway. If successful, you can consider us even."

The man leaned back in his chair, relaxing his aggressive stance. His thoughts penetrated her mind in a far less intimidating manner than his words had fallen upon her ears. "My name is Hypnos. I am the twin of Thanatos. I work for him tonight, not for you." Turning toward his brother, he quipped, "What do you need of me, brother?"

"Make her remember this conversation when she wakes. I have warned her time and again yet she never remembers. Make this seem like a nightmare worse than the one she is currently living. Make this meeting so important to her dormant mind that when she awakes, it is as if she only blinked, losing none of the information she has learned here. After that, her choice will be her own. We will have done our part as we have been charged to do."

Hypnos nodded and smiled. "That will be rather easy, Thanatos. Wish her luck, and I will send her on her way."

Thanatos, without emotion, looked at Jamie who was now fully in a state of shock. He reached his ice cold hand across the table and lightly yet firmly grabbed her chin, causing her to focus directly into the center of his eyes. "We will only meet one more time. You will decide when that will be. Until next time, Jamie."

As his hand let go and started to slide across the table, Jamie's eyes darted wildly toward where Hypnos had been, but he was no longer there. Everything was fading to black as she felt like her body was being pulled backwards into an abyss. She was falling uncontrollably into nothingness with increasing speed.

Jamie took a deep breath as she woke from her sleep, startled for a million different reasons. She remembered everything about the road trip, highway, gas station, inn, Thanatos, and Hypnos. She quickly realized her time was extremely limited as she could hear her boyfriend at the other end of the house, calling for her while destroying things in his path. He was enraged, and she needed to run.

She jammed her feet into shoes that had never been untied since she first laced them years ago and grabbed the emergency bag she had stashed in the back of her closet. Inside she had extra clothes, some non-perishable food, and an extra charger for her phone. She grabbed her wallet off of the dresser along with her cell phone, throwing them into the bag as she headed toward the window. There was not enough time to make it the front or back door before she would have been seen. She snatched the spare car keys off of his dresser beside the window and spotted his wallet, reminding her that she didn't have cash on her. She made a mental note to be sure to stop at an ATM as soon as she was a safe distance away from the house. She didn't want to risk meeting another Momus on her journey. As she heard her boyfriend storming down the hallway toward the bedroom door, Jamie made her final move out of the window. She was in the car and gone before he realized what had happened.

Jamie's new journey began in the middle of a hot July night. She had no time to ponder her decision, but she knew she had made the correct one. Her first step towards making a better life for herself was letting go of an abusive relationship in order to save her own life. Second, calling her parents who had not heard from her in months. She excitedly told them she was driving somewhere safe, to find a better life for herself, knowing that she would only fall in love with someone willing to give to her the kind of love she truly deserved. After hanging up the phone, she was at peace. She knew in her heart happiness and serenity awaited her at the end of her journey. Indeed, when she would inevitably meet Thanatos again, Jamie would have no reason to fear his presence.

16.
Mortar and Men
Chloe Vider

The materials don't matter
brick, mortar, hay, plaster or particle board
all make for the same
a house is not a home
 licking lips and twirling hips
lost in the sound of construction
each hammered nail a symphony
each sweaty shout a dazzling lyric
so much can be found in the mundane
because in the end, everything is made by
Mortar and Men
muscles flexing, the sun rises and sets in their arms
the rain and snow fall from their brows
every piece of the earth is exuded from their skin.

17.
Orange Sky
Jessica Malen

I did not arrive in heaven the day that I died. In fact, I didn't really know how I had arrived where I was. I had no memory of anything regarding my death. I only knew that I was dead. Yet, somehow, I still felt alive.

The first thing I noticed was the brilliant orange of the sky, as though the sun longed to set but it couldn't. The clouds were perfectly formed, like little cotton balls that had been pulled apart, stretched and tossed into the air. I was lying underneath a cover of wildflowers and all I could see was sky. I stood up slowly and looked all around me— I was completely and utterly alone. I was in (what appeared to be) an infinite meadow full of tall green grass. The grass felt cool and damp beneath my bare feet. I wandered aimlessly through the field, touching the tops of the long, slender pieces of grass. A supple wind moved gracefully through the meadow, making the grass sway as if music was playing.

I felt dazed. It was as though I had been asleep for hundreds of years and I was just waking up. I stared up at the sky and screamed. It wasn't even in anger, just out of frustration. I yelled to no one, to infinity or maybe to god. I didn't really know, since every perception of "heaven" that I had was completely wrong up so far. I never imagined that when I actually died, I would be really alone.

The next thing that I noticed was that there was no day. No week. No month. No year. No time. The orange of the sky and the fluffy white clouds never changed from the way they were.

I lay back down in the grass and closed my eyes. I wasn't tired. I tried to think. Back, back, back to before.

What was 'before'? Who was I really? My name was Sophie. I lived in New York City. I was seventeen years old. I could have been anyone. I hadn't even been able to vote or go to college yet. My biggest accomplishment was making enough money as a babysitter for an Upper East Side family to save up and buy a car; which broke down immediately after its purchase.

I could feel my memory coming back in tiny jolts of electricity. I remembered my parents. Their recent divorce had caused my dad to move across the country to be with his new family and I hadn't talked to him since. I remembered how everything would be alright by the end of the day, at least it usually was. I thought about my little sister Casey. She had just turned seven and we threw a zoo-animal themed party for her with lots of balloons. All of her little friends came dressed as different animals but she was the only monkey in the whole group. "Look at me, Sophie! Look at me!" she had been standing on our back porch with her arms outstretched towards me waiting for a hug. Tears stung my eyes and I closed them trying to capture the vivid colors of my past life that flashed inside my mind.

When I opened my eyes I noticed that everything was still the same, except for a large tree with huge green leaves at the far end of the field. It hadn't been there when I had first closed my eyes. What was this place? Magical trees just growing out of nowhere?

For whatever reason, the tree made me really angry. If this was where I was supposed to spend eternity alone, then shouldn't someone ask for my consent to put a tree in here?

I stalked over towards the tree. I would show him, god or whoever sent me to this terrible place. I wondered if this could be hell; but I knew I hadn't been a bad person. I had always listened, obeyed and followed the rules: I did what I supposed to do.

The tree actually grew to me when I began to walk towards it. The branches twisted, turned and stretched in my direction, calling me to it. Light green leaves bloomed and unfolded out of nowhere. Damn tree. I stopped walking and waited for it to reach me.

When the tree appeared to have stopped growing, I was completely underneath a canopy of branches. I noticed how cool the shade from the tree felt against my skin. The sun shone through the new leaves as though they were the stained glass windows of a cathedral. I slumped down against the trunk. I had never seen this kind of a tree before; it looked as though all of the bark had been stripped away. I ran my hands over the trunk. It felt like a polished table.

"Do you like it?" a muffled musical voice called suddenly. It sounded like a small child.

I jumped up in a terrified surprise. I looked around me but I didn't see anyone. I was such a mess. I must've been so lonely that I imagined voices. I sat back down against the tree and put my head in my hands.

"Up here," the voice beckoned again.

I looked above me into the tree where a small boy with sandy blonde hair sat smiling. His bare feet were dangling over the branch. He wore a shirt with a fire truck on it. In the truck was a little black dog wearing a firefighter hat riding in the front of the truck. He also had on a pair of faded green shorts.

"Who are you?" I managed to spit out, bewildered.

"My name's Luc," he smiled and hopped down from the tree. Jeez, he was so small, probably only around three years old.

"You look scared," he giggled, "You don't have to be."

I shut my mouth because I noticed that it had been hanging open. I wasn't scared, just surprised. Besides, he was adorable, I couldn't be afraid of a little boy.

He seemed to sense this and gestured for me to sit down next to him. I did so, slowly.

"So," he said, "What's your name?" He crossed his legs Indian style and looked up at me patiently waiting for an answer.

"You're not some kind of demon are you? This isn't a trick?" I didn't want to offend him, but I had to ask.

"I don't think so?" He looked confused. He had such a cute face. He reminded me so much of my little sister Casey. I missed her so much. I noticed this was the first time that I had felt that emotion: missing someone. Until now, I hadn't missed anyone at all. But I missed Casey.

"My name is Sophie." I whispered as a few tears rolled down my cheek. I hated being stuck in this stupid place.

I felt Luc's hand on my cheek as he gently wiped away my tears. I looked down at him as he smiled up at me. He was so innocent.

"This isn't heaven," Luc sat back against the tree.

"What?" I asked looking into his brown eyes. They were so warm and friendly.

"It's not heaven," Luc repeated with a smile, as if this was a good thing, "This is the waiting place. To wait."

"To wait?" I repeated.

"Yes, for people who are special," as he said this he tugged on his little red shirt, adjusting it.

"What is that supposed to mean?"

"You'll see," he smiled and looked off to his right, "Let's go for a walk. I want to show you something." He jumped up and skipped out from under the shade of the tall green tree, and into the warmth of the sun.

"Where are we going?" I called to Luc, who was now dancing through the field. I could only see his little blond head bounce up and down from time to time as he moved.

"Come on!" his little voice called to me.

"There's nowhere else to go!" I called to him. I had already been everywhere there was to go in this endless field of nothing.

"That's what you think," he called back as he continued to run ahead, his bright red shirt standing in stark contrast with the grass.

I followed him anyways.

I caught up to him eventually, and he giggled and took off running in another direction. I chased him around in circles because that seemed to be what he wanted. I noticed how gentle the wind felt against my face, how warm the sky felt; then music began to fill the air. It wasn't a loud noise; it was more like faint wind chimes: a melody created from the grass, the tree and the soil.

I felt an overpowering bond to the ground as Luc grabbed my hands. We spun in circles faster, faster. I saw no look of alarm on his face, only pure bliss. He giggled throwing his head back and told me to hold on.

Surprisingly, I didn't feel dizzy at all. In the center of where we were spinning, a plant began to grow. It began as a small seedling with only a few leaves. Then it grew bigger and bigger until it grew into a sapling. Slowly, it became a baby tree with sweet smelling blossoms. Around and around we went, until the tree was fully grown and there were cherries falling from its branches. Unexpectedly, Luc let go of my hands and I stumbled backwards into the grass.

"This," he said as he ran over to where I had fell, "is life."

"A tree?" I was confused.

"It grows, does it not?"

I shrugged.

"So therefore: it lives. It is alive." He laughed and reached up to pluck a ripe, red cherry off of the tree and handed it to me.

I looked up at him and he nodded, so I bit into the red fruit. It was unlike anything I had ever tasted in my life. Succulent, rich, sweet and overpowering. I felt immediately happy and light. I grinned at Luc as he reached for my hand.

"You know the only way that you'll ever be happy, Sophie?" Luc asked me as he led me back towards the tree.

I popped another cherry into my mouth, "How's that?"

"Love. Salvation lies in love." He smiled the sweetest smile that I had ever seen.

"Sometimes I feel I don't deserve to be loved, though, like I'm not good enough for anyone." I felt myself opening up to this little boy without hesitation.

Luc only smiled at me as we paused in the middle of the field. The gentle breeze swirled around us, blowing the sweet smell of cherries through my hair. My arms and legs felt warm as the sun kissed them with far away lips.

"Everyone deserves to be loved," he said to me.

"I wish I felt that way." I looked around at all of the grass swaying in the breeze.

"It's beautiful here, isn't it?" Luc asked as we began to walk again.

"It really is. I wish that Earth looked like this." The orange of the sky, the green of the grass, it felt incredibly immaculate.

"It does," he said matter-of-factly.

"No," I said glancing towards the tree we were approaching, "Maybe you didn't notice because you're so young, but Earth doesn't look like this, Luc."

"Maybe you didn't notice because you were so old."

When we reached the tree, Luc let go of my hand and grabbed the lowest branch and swung himself onto it, like a baby monkey.

"Come on Sophie!" he called to me.

"I can't climb trees." I told him hesitantly.

"Of *course* you can!" he laughed.

I really couldn't though. The last time that I had climbed a tree, I was ten years old and I ended up with a broken leg. I had a cast on that prevented me from swimming all summer.

"You were a kid once weren't you?" He called again. I didn't know if he was actually asking me this or if he meant it as a joke.

I grabbed the first branch and pulled myself up into the tree. I couldn't see Luc, but I could hear him humming a little tune above me and I laughed.

I finally reached the top and Luc grabbed my hand. He helped steady me as I poked my head through the leaves of the tree.

"Hello again," Luc greeted me. He was sitting on a large, sturdy looking branch with a clear view of the entire meadow. He motioned for me to join him. So I did.

"Look around you," he told me once I was sitting next to him. I still was gripping his tiny hand inside mine. I looked around us. I could see the entire field, even the cherry tree. Beyond it was a glistening blue lake and a vast, rocky mountain range.

"When did those get here?" I gasped. I really must be crazy!

"They were always here," Luc said turning to me and smiling, "You just weren't ready to see them."

"I wasn't?" I was amazed that this strange little boy knew so much.

"Nope," he giggled, "You were too blinded by anger to see the beauty around you."

I didn't see why this was so funny, but I couldn't help laughing anyway.

I don't know how long we sat up in the tree, but it was a long time. Days? Months? Maybe years. I would never be able to tell.

"How did you die, Luc?" I asked after a while.

He looked up at me grinning, "Cancer. My mother was angry with god, I think, after I died. I used to visit to check up on my family all the time."

"Really? You can do that?" I asked, my eyes widening.

"Of course," he laughed.

"Why would she be angry with god though?" I wondered if my own mother was angry with god.

"She didn't have anyone to blame for my death. Parents blame themselves, because they're supposed to protect their children. When something happens that's out of their control, parents need someone, or somewhere, to take out their frustration. But it wasn't anyone's fault that I died. It's just a disease, I was sick for a long time. I wasn't the first to die from cancer and I won't be the last."

I just looked at him for a while. He had his legs crossed and was wiggling his little pink toes.

"I don't remember how I died," I said despondently. I wished that I could remember. I wanted to have something to share with this little boy, since it seemed to be the only thing we had in common.

"Then maybe you never really died," he cocked his head to the side, as though he was pondering a serious thought.

"If I didn't die then why am I here in this...waiting place?" I didn't even know if that was possible to not be dead, but be dead?

"It's for special people. I never said it was for *dead* people, Sophie. Maybe this place is for people who aren't meant to die," he laughed a silly laugh as though I should have known this all along.

"Oh…" What was that supposed to mean? "Are you supposed to be my guardian angel or something?"

He smiled at me and squeezed my hand, "We don't have guardian angels, Sophie, just people who love us."

Suddenly Luc let go of my hand and stood up. He tugged his shirt off over his tiny blond head and tucked it into the pocket of his green shorts. He stretched his little tan arms above his head, and grinned at me. All of a sudden, two beautiful white, feathered wings sprouted from his back then he leapt off of the tree and into the air.

"Hey!" I called after him. He couldn't just leave me here alone.

He turned back at me laughing, "Come on, Sophie!"

There wasn't anything funny about this.

"Yeah, right. I can climb a tree Luc, but I can't fly."

"Of course you can!"

"No Luc. I can't. I'll kill myself."

"But you're dead!"

"I thought you said I wasn't dead…"

"Well, we're going to find out. Jump!" his brown eyes gleamed curiously. He then turned and fluttered off towards the mountains. His wings were definite against the orange of the sky.

I took one last breath and looked all around me, I took in all of the beauty that this place held, and then I leapt into the air.

"Wake up." A distant voice called to me, "Sophie, wake up."

I wiped my eyes. What a strange dream.

"Yeah, I'm up." I opened my eyes only to see a sterile white hospital room surrounding me. My mother was standing at my bedside gripping my hand, her eyes were red. She looked exhausted and older than I had remembered. I glanced to my right and felt someone holding my other hand. Casey.

"I thought you were gonna die, dork," she whispered with tears brimming her eyes.

I was stuck in the hospital for the next month. Apparently I had been in a pretty rough car accident. The driver had been drunk and I went through the windshield.

Every day, I got to go down the kids' room to watch TV or do puzzles in the Pediatric ICU because the one on my floor was under reconstruction. Having two broken legs didn't leave me a lot of room for things to do and staring out the window everyday into a parking lot got old pretty quick.

On one particular day, I wheeled myself down to the kids' room in my wheelchair and flipped the TV to some fashion channel. I stared blankly at the screen. I was just starting to doze off to sleep when a little voice called to me.

"Hello," it said.

I turned to see a little boy with a bald-head coloring at the miniature plastic table in the corner of the room. He had on blue hospital pajamas just like me.

"Hey," I called back without really looking up from the TV. I glanced at him from the corner of my eye. He looked like a cancer patient. There were a lot of cancer patients on this floor of the hospital. I probably shouldn't have been down there, but I needed to get out of my room.

After a few minutes he dragged his IV stand beside me and held the picture he had been working on in front of me.

It was of a beautiful field under what looked like an infinite orange sky. My eyes widened and I stared at him.

He beamed, and despite the pale, sickly color of his skin, and the painful look in his eyes, he managed to look happy and at peace.

"I'm Luc," he smiled.

He reached for my hand and I took it.

18.
Oriama Eviscoma
Dennis K. Hausker

Dawn approached as the bright red orb peeked over the distant horizon pushing back the stygian blackness of night. It was a new day signaling the birth of more than a solar cycle; it was the first time his eyes opened on the world.

Initially, it was disorienting, the increasing light flooding his sense of sight, a first experience as a living being. His first response was blinking, not a difficult act, but an accomplishment nonetheless for one alone without a teacher.

Blinking again, closing his lids, and then reopening them constituted progress.

His awareness expanded rapidly as he realized there was more to him than eyes. A thought occurred in his mind, unbidden. Move.

He began to rock his head back and forth. It was possible to do, but difficult. The difficulty annoyed him so he tried harder and managed to move farther, but still he felt restrained.

Restraint wasn't a condition he would tolerate so he increased his efforts of movement.

As he concentrated on the first goal of his life, his efforts stimulated further awareness; he consisted of more than eyes and a head. New sensations alerted him to other parts of his being. Those parts also responded to his wish which, at this point singularly, was movement.

Forcing his entirety into fighting against the annoyance, the feeling of restraint, it triggered more responses in his body. His mind was a sponge soaking in everything and self-awareness grew rapidly. Everyplace, he felt the sensation of restraint and it stirred him to new efforts. With a force of will, he pulled all of his body against the barrier, but this time with great determination, and force.

There was another sense, he could also hear, and what he heard was a sucking sound as incrementally he moved to sit up. Freeing his head and then bending upward half of his body he felt momentary nausea and vertigo. Looking at the sight after his distress passed, he saw ooze covering him, residue of what? He didn't know the answer. From his seated position, he looked at the planet for the first time and saw vast rugged mountains far in the distance, nearby forests all around him, and in the sky far up he saw movement, tiny specks of something flitting about. It generated curiosity. He could only note these sights, having no frame of reference yet to comprehend any significance in his new world.

Looking again at his body, he saw the lower half was still immersed in the goo. Levering himself, he struggled to his feet, unsteady and off balance. The imprint of where he'd lain was gone completely as the viscous substance flowed together leaving no trace.

Taking his first step to move out of the pool, it was a short distance to the edge. Once he arrived at the barrier and stepped out, the tingle in his body dissipated, the goo was suddenly gone off of him, and his mind flooded with memories, knowledge of a before. With that knowledge and those memories he received another awakening, his emotions. Instantly, he felt terrible pangs of loss, losses too painful to bear. He hadn't been alone in that 'before.' There were other people, important people to him. There had been... family.

Discovering he could make sounds with a voice, the first sound he made was a wail, gut wrenching agony at his painful past.

His mind punished him with a vivid replay of his last memory.

War had ravaged his civilization to the point of extinction. Fighting a delaying action against a relentless and pitiless enemy, they'd tried to save the loved ones. The sight of the explosions as the ships tried to flee drove him to suicidal rage. Charging those foes to end a life without those he cherished led to...what? He couldn't remember, nor could he determine where he was, at this moment. Nothing was familiar at all in his new surroundings.

Without a conscious plan and no place to go; he started to walk, his pace getting stronger and surer with each step. His painful feelings shackled him with hopelessness. Was there a point now?

Heading for the closest edge of the forest for no real reason, he plodded along. Suddenly as he looked, forms emerged from amongst the trees, a group of people. He continued walking toward them, whether it was safe to do so, he didn't care.

As they drew close, the group stared at him in awe.

He paused in a daze. These people, there was something familiar about them. A female broke off from the group and approached him cautiously.

"Oriama? Husband?"

Words filled his mind, instantaneous and full recall of a language from before. "That's a name, my name?"

"Don't you recognize me, Oriama? I'm Leta, your wife."

"Wife? I had a wife, but I remember utter pain. I lost her, and my little children. My soul bleeds for her."

"I'm not lost, nor are our children. We escaped the onslaught, but you were grievously injured. Your brave actions attacking the enemy saved us all. We brought you here to this new planet, but you didn't survive so we buried you in the ground. How is this possible you stand before me, alive again? You look... changed."

"I awoke in that lake of goo."

"What lake of goo?"

He turned around and saw it was gone. Only dry ground in grassland remained.

"Your grave was there. Daily, we come here to honor you."

"I, eh... I don't understand what happened to me."

They heard the howl of predators in the distance.

"It isn't wise to be out now but even in the light there is danger. We need to get you some clothes." He realized he was naked for the first time.

Leta put an arm around his waist. "Come this way, it's not far."

Walking through the woods on an animal trail he saw the wooden walls surrounding the settlement just ahead. The protective barrier didn't strike him as adequate. With each moment, and with each step, he felt more a living person and a man named Oriama.

Men had gone ahead to explain the miracle of him, seemingly returned from the dead. They had clothes brought out so he could enter the village unashamed. Seeing his son and daughters warmed his heart. It was like a door opening bringing back his old life and assuaging his torment. Grasping them in a firm embrace, he felt joy and renewal at the miraculous, though unexplained, renaissance. Looking at his wife's tear filled eyes, all his love was magically brought back to him again.

"Atha, son," he muttered, putting his hands on his son's shoulders.

"Father? What happened? You died?"

Shaking his head, Oriama shrugged. "A miracle."

His little daughters stood hesitate, their eyes betraying fear. He put out his arms to them.

"It's me, girls. Laia, Kirsta, come to me, please."

They glanced at their mother who nodded before they moved into his arms. Hugging them firmly, Oriama closed his eyes. "My dearest darlings, I love you so much." Savoring the exquisite love of a parent for a child, he felt emotions well up and nearly bring him to tears holding his three dear ones. It struck him as odd his wife didn't join the group embrace.

The healer approached and eyed him clinically. She was standing nearby, a matronly gray haired woman, wise and thoughtful, expertly appraising him.

"I can't control my feelings," Oriama ventured. "I love them so much, it hurts."

"This isn't a concern. It's common after severe traumas to feel emotional spikes. You have no memories of what happened to you?"

"I do not. I have memories of what was, but in a way, I'm not that person I was any longer. Does that make sense?"

"This is new ground. None of us have answers to the mystery. Obviously, none of our people have ever come back from dying."

"My last memory was a bright light; I thought it was the explosions in the battle killing me."

"You survived the battle, though you were grievously wounded. The enemy was driven away long enough for us to come back for you and then escape. Our people scattered fleeing in ships going in every direction to seek new homes and safety in new galaxies. We decided small numbers wouldn't draw notice from the dark ones. Thus far, we seem to be safe here, at least from our former perils. Life here has dangers of its own."

"You said I didn't survive. You buried me?"

"This is true, my friend. What it means, I have no ideas. Obviously, some force was at work on you. There's no residual sign of your injuries at all that I can see. Your body, or perhaps I should say, your new body looks like us, somewhat, but at the same time different. The hue of your skin is lighter; your musculature is thicker, more powerful looking. Your facial features seem altered. Your eye color is changed from brown to hazel. Your hair color is much lighter also."

Oriama looked at the healer. She seemed hesitant to say more. Her facial expression was one of regret.

"What is it?"

"I hope you can take this in the right spirit. We want to be sure, well... that you're not a danger. I'm sorry to say that, but we're a small community and can't endure losses of our people and still hope to survive. Life is tenuous enough trying to eke out sufficient food supplies in an unforgiving environment trying to feed us and face the deadly perils with the considerable number of predators living around us. If there's another side to your return, a dark side, we need to determine that right away."

"I understand. It's not a problem for me."

Oriama noted discomfited looks not only on the healer's face but his wife and all of the others standing around watching him. His children hugged him tightly. "There's more, tell me all of it."

"Our needs as a community, eh...this will be difficult for you to hear, required that there couldn't be people not contributing to the greater whole." The healer paused.

"I don't know what that means? What are you saying?"

"We're under populated. That issue had to be addressed."

She paused again. Oriama merely waited. "You were dead. Your wife didn't wish it, but we asked she curtail her mourning period and take another partner. All of our women understand they must bear more children. I'm sorry; I know this is a shock."

Oriama was speechless. On a day of firsts, this wasn't one which he anticipated, or wanted. Looking at Leta, he saw her emotional conflict in her eyes. Neither of them spoke. After a moment, he stated the obvious. "You have another husband?"

"I'm sorry. We couldn't know you'd come back to life. I carry his child."

Oriama grimaced. This was a new pain of spirit, his wife carrying another man's child. With the greatest difficultly, he tried to say the right thing. "I don't blame you, Leta. What I don't understand is why I was brought back."

"I feel the need to ask your forgiveness, Oriama."

"Why? As you said, you couldn't have known. I won't cause a problem for you. This other man will have his child with you. That child needs its own father to help in raising it, and its mother."

He noticed a grim faced man watching him closely, a stranger. Oriama fought his rush of anger. Feeling his emotions roiling about, jealousy and anger percolated dangerously just below the surface. Rather than allow it to create an incident, Oriama got up and turned his back. Being the better man was so difficult to endure. "I'd like to see the settlement and perhaps go out into the forest to acclimate to my new home." He spoke softly to mask his true feelings.

"Oriama, I'm so sorry. Please."

He couldn't look at his wife. More accurately, was she his former wife? It was beyond his endurance to stand any further in this crucible of emotional punishment.

"Father, may I walk with you?" Atha asked him. He nodded and walked away with his son, never looking back.

The pain of the disclosure was worse than a blade plunged into his heart. Optimism disappeared from his life in an instant. The 'love of his life' belonged to another man and he was helpless to do anything about it.

"His name is Toran," Atha explained as they walked.

"Is he good to you and your mother?"

"He is good, but father, I never saw him in place of you. I wish to live with you."

Oriama glanced at him and smiled ruefully. "Thank you, son, but I have no wish to cause your mother pain. She loves you and needs you also. Perhaps we can arrange to spend some time together away from your family, you and me."

"You're my family."

"I appreciate that, but with my sudden presence, I could be an issue causing discord in your new family. I don't want that, and you don't need it in your life. Your sisters need their big brother watching out for them. This other man, Toran, he will feel threatened by me. I should have stayed buried in the ground."

"No, that's not right. We're your children. My sisters feel just as I do. We would all live with you, our real father."

Oriama wrestled with the troubling issue bereft of a good solution. The love and loyalty of his child expressed in such passionate terms meant a great deal at that difficult time. Going outside the settlement walls into the forest, his instincts took over. None of his former training, experiences, and forest lore was lost to him. He was competent and he was lethal as ever as an elite caliber soldier. "What have you learned about this world, Atha? What do I need to know?"

"The most fearful of the predators hunt at night, but there's danger in the light also. Cats are huge, agile, and fast, other larger creatures are hard to describe other than nightmares come to life. Seeing them usually means dying moments later. They seem to avoid our settlement generally, but from time to time, they've come close and they're terrifying. Some are big enough I wonder if they could easily knock down our wooden walls. If they ever ran out of food, I think we would quickly be their next prey."

Oriama walked in silence, looking around at various topographical features, learning the layout of the land and fixing it in his mind. That's what soldiers did, assess the surroundings and prepare contingencies. Most critically, be prepared for anything and everything.

"You have something in mind, father. I know you. What is it?"

"It may be best if I establish a home out here, separate from your settlement."

"Why, why would you do that?"

"I realize this is difficult for you, son. If I were to live back there amongst them, I would be subject to the same rules and requirements. Pairing me with another woman to impregnate while your mother is with this other man, I couldn't live such a life. Perhaps I've been reborn as a selfish man, too heedless of the needs of others or the good of the community. I don't know. I can only say that this is reality for me."

"Then I'll come join you. Mother has my sisters. You have nothing. I can't abide your being further wrongly punished by the choices of others. You were our greatest warrior. You sacrificed your life and personally saved us. It isn't right that you should be made to suffer in this way. I feel like driving Toran away."

"Son, I can't tell you how grateful I am for your words and thoughts, but I repeat, I don't want your mother to suffer. As galling as it is, I must tell you not to blame Toran. He's not at fault here."

"I won't concede this point, father. I can live without Toran's influence and his guidance. I will follow you to become a man you would be proud of, a man who does great things in his life. Who better to hone me into iron? I'll accept no other."

Oriama was greatly moved and a part of him was gratified. Exposing his son to mortal peril here, though, was a powerful deterrent to accepting his son's emotionally skewed vision of a future life together. Whether Oriama could successfully live apart from the safety and numbers in the settlement and survive the beasts was an unanswered question. On this dangerous world, great skills might not guarantee a long life. They forged ahead in silence for a time.

Oriama thought about the "miracle." There was no memory he could call up. Whatever force touched him, or if there were other beings at work, he had no way to discover what happened. It was impossible; there was no technology which could accomplish it. That was the undeniable fact. Beyond that fact, the compelling question for Oriama was "why?"

Atha's face was a mask of concern. It evoked Oriama's turbulent feelings, but there too, was there an answer? His son wouldn't accept a return to the reconfigured family and it appeared his relationship with Toran would erode if Oriama forced him back there.

The terrible news was shocking, but what jumped out at him was how Leta held back. Making no gesture toward her former husband, seemingly showing no desire to resume their marriage, it devastated him. Perhaps Toran was a better man, a better husband, a change Leta favored. If it was true, that was the most damning affront of all and a guarantee he couldn't live among them in their settlement. It made him wonder about his former married life, if it was a mirage of bliss solely of his own imagining.

As he walked, his feelings were evolving. Anger simmered like a defense mechanism to protect him from further emotional harm. The thought of talking with Leta to understand, or to resolve the matter, it struck him as pointless. His friends, his former life, they were gone, and in the settlement he was anathema. At least, that was the unwarranted conclusion he came to in his own skewed view of reality at that point in time. Recently returned to life, it was another aspect of his not fully being the same person he was previously. Emotions were far more volatile in this incarnation.

"Father, there's a significant place just ahead. It's at the edge of this forest. I tell you this because it's very dangerous. Animal trails converge because waters of a large lake is nearby and also broad meadows with grasses to graze. For the predators, even in the daylight, it's easy meat. I think if we wander in there, we take too great a risk."

"I trust your judgment, Atha, but I want to see the place at least once. Is there a place we can view the area from safety?"

Atha pondered the question. "There are no elevated points, so the next place for a view would be scaling a tree. That might seem safe enough, but some predators pounce from trees. They climb quickly and easily. We could be trapped without an exit. We would be the easy meat."

Oriama chuckled. "I understand, son. Perhaps seeing this place you speak of can wait for another day." In spite of the dismal circumstances of his first day, spending time with his son proved to be therapeutic, a balm for his soul. At a time where he could see nothing positive to focus on for his future, it was a rare comfort.

"I'll ask you again, what are you planning?"

"At this point, I don't have a master plan. My first decision is; do I want to survive? I could simply walk into the jaws of a beast and end this misery. If I decide to continue on, I can only go day to day, dealing with this situation like I would in a war. First, I need to fashion weapons, then I need a place where I'd live, and then to fully immerse into this world, learn all the creatures and establish my place within their realm. Simplistic, I know, but I've usually found the simplest way is often the best choice to make."

"Father, I want to explain more to you."

Oriama looked at the distressed look on Atha's face.

"You weren't given the entire story of their survival plan. It isn't only that any woman who can bear children is expected to allow impregnation. The leaders decided they need to diversify the gene pool, so each new child they birth would come from a different father. Toran wouldn't be mother's mate for life. It isn't a replacement marriage. They plan to raise the children outside of the conventional family structures with group arrangements. Children reside with their mothers, but the whole community shares in raising and mentoring them. That way, the confusing situations of many fathers in every family won't be an issue. Men stay with women until they've created and birthed the child. At least that's their idea for a viable society. Supposedly, once enough children are born and reach maturity, at that time they'd consider returning to more traditional family structures. My sisters would be expected to birth children when they reach puberty and can sustain pregnancy to term."

"I wasn't a scientist. I can't dispute their theories, but I don't like it. Perhaps it's necessary to their communal survival, but it's demeaning and destructive of our moral views with taking all of these different partners. There's no love taken into consideration, and I think it's easy to see women in unflattering lights. If they're nothing more than incubators subject to...well. My opinion is these radical plans can have unanticipated consequences. What I saw in your mother's eyes when she told me she was pregnant, it was chilling. The lifetime we shared together, it didn't seem to have any impact on her. It was unnerving. What sort of people come out of the other end of this experiment? Even factoring in the shock of my return and her possible repulsion toward an unknown entity, I believe the issues I'm talking about are already there."

"I understand. I've been told I'm physically capable of fathering children, so when the next pregnant woman gives birth and is free, I would be her next consort. Their ideal would be that eventually every man fathers a child with every woman in the settlement."

Oriama grimaced.

"I don't feel right about it, father. I guess I agree about the moral issue. I want to choose a wife, like you and mother did, to share a life and grow old together."

Mulling over the new disclosure, Oriama asked, "Was there no dissention to this plan?"

"There was discussion, but it was clear no one had a better plan. Some people voiced objections, but it was along the lines we're talking about, moral decay, seeing women in a different light, as objects for male attentions rather than as people. Do you understand?"

"Completely."

"In her defense, mother was vocal with her concerns. It wasn't so much with her rejecting taking another man since you were...dead, but, with my sisters. At their young ages now, it's hard to imagine their future when they're old enough, going into a pool of baby makers that every male would eventually know, in that way."

Oriama scowled at the prospect.

"Father, if you choose to live apart, there will be no one else to stand against this arrangement they're forcing on us. None have the personal strength to counter this...wrong. The idea of being with other men's wives, it bothers me a great deal."

"It bothers me also, son."

"Can you turn away from what will happen to my sisters, your daughters?"

"I can't turn away from your mother being used like this. As we talk, I'm starting to believe I need to act, though I still have no answer to the community dilemma. I understand about having a viable population base to be able to reproduce successfully, but this way?"

"Perhaps that's a part of why you were brought back?"

"I have many questions about that, but no answers."

Turning around a bend in the trail, both men froze as on the path staring at them was a huge cat. Having just made a kill, it eyed them savagely. "No quick moves, son. Slowly back up but don't turn your back to it."

The predator growled a deep frightening warning. As an old habit, Oriama reached for his weapon holster, but there was nothing. That was his former life. Only Atha had a bow and arrows. With the limited numbers of modern weapons and ammunition they salvaged in their escape, those weapons were reserved for the men of the settlement.

"Can you use that thing?"

"Yes, sir."

"Notch an arrow, but be careful in doing it."

Each step they took backwards created more distance for the cat to cover if it charged, but neither man felt safer. Once they reached a point out of sight of the cat, they hustled away. Fortunately, the cat chose not to follow.

"Do you see what I say, Father? Even a simple stroll is fraught with danger on this world. If we'd arrived a few minutes sooner, we could have been the dead prey the cat dragged away to feed on."

"I need to make my weapons now."

Again, expertly looking around the area, Oriama selected the right wood to fashion his own bow. Fortuitously, Atha had extra string for his father's bow, and shared his supply of arrows.

"I'll make more arrows of my own, thank you, son. I've decided to return to the settlement. Even if my residence there is temporary, at this point it's necessary because it's too dangerous out here without a good plan, a location for a safe place to live, and sufficient supplies. The social issues are the other factor. I thought my wife discarded me, but from what you're saying, that's not necessarily the case. Certainly, I care about the lives of my daughters, so perhaps I need to compromise and not give my own bruised feelings too much power in guiding my decisions."

"Good, I was hoping you'd change your mind. Whatever you do, I'm with you completely. If you later move out here into the forest, I will accompany you."

Oriama shrugged, struggling with conflicting emotions. It was gratifying to receive his son's loyalty, but that didn't assuage the pain of Leta in the arms of another man.

He was far more cautious on his return trip. They heard movement not so far away from the path, but no creatures came out to accost them.

Walking back inside the walls, Oriama pondered how best to handle this difficult social situation.

"Father, come to our house. If he doesn't like it, I don't care. Mother doesn't belong to him, regardless of the edict."

"That would be a difficult thing, son. The reasons I gave are still true."

"I care about our family and that doesn't include him."

"Atha, don't make him into our enemy because he's not. I'll try to forge a fair way to deal with the problem. That won't involve fighting and driving him away. I will, however, make it clear to him that my children are not within his scope, and I'll talk to my wife about her responsibility for our daughters in her care."

It sounded reasonable, explaining it to Atha, and it seemed doable, but when they got to the house, Oriama felt anxiety and nearly second guessed his decision.

Atha opened the door before he could leave, so he went inside. Laia and Kirsta saw him and exclaimed. "Father, you came home." They rushed into his embrace and again he was swept with love for his little darlings. Leta walked into the room from the kitchen along with Toran. She looked shocked, Toran looked angry.

"I hope this visit isn't inconvenient. I've talked with my son and come to some decisions. Will you hear me?"

"Of course," Leta replied. Toran said nothing.

Oriama noticed the baby bump. He hadn't paid attention to it before. It stoked his darker emotions which he fought to control. Additionally, Toran had an arm around her waist, eyeing Oriama with challenge in his eyes.

"Atha has explained the life you've all chosen for your settlement. Obviously, I wasn't here to have my say. Whatever transpired is water under the bridge. I'm only looking at what occurs from this point forward. I'm told each male consort resides with a woman until the birth of the child at which point they rotate to other women thereby maximizing the widest pool of genetic diversity."

"That's correct, Oriama."

"I made some wrong assumptions before. It was such a shock I just didn't handle it well. This is partially why I've come back now. I want to say to you, Toran. I'll honor what I said. Your mating with my wife can't be reversed. She carries your child so I won't try to move into this house with the strife it would cause. However, I won't forsake my children, or my wife for that matter. They will be welcome to visit me whenever they choose. That would include my wife. As far as this reproductive plan, I haven't come to a decision about it, or what to do. I'm not going to join in with fertilizing the settlement females. I believe my son is of a similar mindset."

Leta's face contorted with emotion. Tears formed at the edges. Spontaneously, she came over to embrace her husband. Oriama felt almost vindicated after his bout of self-doubt and rejection.

"I'm so sorry," she whispered over and over again, sobbing softly. "I thought I'd lost you."

"Never, that could never happen, my wife."

She sobbed on his shoulder.

"Be at peace, I really don't blame you. If you still want me, we'll deal with this distraction of the pregnancy."

"I would move in with you now, Oriama. You know that."

"I realize it isn't allowed under these current settlement rules. His retaining husband type rights to you and...well, the conjugal things during this period, I hate it but I'll bide my time. The instant the baby is born, though, I'll be knocking on your door."

She chuckled and squeezed him tightly.

Oriama was finally in the loving embrace of his wife, and it meant more than anything to him. His children stood nearby smiling at having both parent's returned in their lives.

Toran, grimaced and brooded. Oriama turned his head. "Is this going to be a problem for you, what I've just said?"

"No. You said you'd honor the law. She's mine and I will continue our life together, to the fullest."

"I advise you to remember, there will be a time afterwards. Don't do something foolish which we'll all regret later. I don't mean it as a warning, just friendly advice. It may be your law, but you're trespassing on my wife and family. I would take a dim view of such mistakes."

Toran hadn't been one of the soldiers, he was nowhere near to the physical size of Oriama and had none of the military training. Toran had never fought in the wars and certainly he hadn't saved civilization like Oriama. Posing a challenge was the last thing he could do. Any idea to woo and win Leta away from her husband was doomed for failure.

"You need not hurry away, husband. You're welcome in this house."

"I'll stay for a brief time, but I need to go to find my own place somewhere in the settlement. As I said, you can bring the children there anytime. I would hope you will."

"You said earlier you handled this badly, but I did also. When I first saw you, I burned with shame about being pregnant with Toran's baby."

"About that, I think we should both move on. All of that is behind us. I would have liked things to be otherwise, but we can look forward to afterwards. What's ahead is what's important now."

"I feel so much better that you understand the truth and we have peace between us. I'm hopeful, not only that you're here for me, but what you mean for the viability our fragile settlement. We're at risk on a daily basis. There's no one better to move us to a stronger footing."

"I hope you're right. I'll do what I can about our livelihood, but I'm driven to discover what happened to me. I heard what the healer said about her fears of if I might pose a future threat. I wish to know that answer too. I can only assume there's some force, or people, responsible for returning me to life. I'll search out the truth. I can't afford not to."

Oriama sat down to a brief meal. He tried to talk with Toran to reduce the friction. Toran remained moody so it was only partially successful, a one sided attempt. Leta ignored Toran's reticence and chatted brightly with her re-born husband. If there were worries on her part, she didn't show it. Finally, Oriama left them to do his business. Atha accompanied him and wouldn't stay behind.

The council had already made arrangements for a place for Oriama. He had no belongings to move, so his first task was with making weaponry. Obtaining metal blades within the settlement, Oriama fashioned a throwing spear and he made handles for knives. The metal worker later provided him with a long blade for a sword. The council offered him modern weapons but he declined in favor of primitive weaponry. As he created weapons for himself, he also made additional ones for his son. Once armed, they sparred, practiced and trained nearly constantly. Going into the forest to hunt was their other main activity. Atha retained his father's genetics and with the rigorous and constant training, he grew into his man's body rapidly. His broad powerful shoulders were similar to his father's.

With time, Oriama's hunting forays and his martial lifestyle drew some men, mostly former soldiers, to follow him. Following with Oriama's views, the settlement mandates were lesser priorities to this newly honed corps. Though all of the men had already 'performed their duties' with the womenfolk, they didn't spend time in those houses fulfilling husband roles with other men's wives. The corps continued to attract more men.

The hunting parties improved their skills with primitive weapons to save ammunition for the few modern weapons. Increasing their familiarity of the forest animal patterns and habits, they supplied four times the meat prior to Oriama's arrival, averting starvation for the community.

Atha was a proud participant in the corps but unfortunately, he didn't control his disdain for Toran. It meant he seldom slept at home; rather he stayed at his father's home in lieu of serious arguments. Leta didn't want to be put in the position to defend and safeguard Toran. Atha's new incarnation was a strong and dangerous young man with a quick temper when it came to Toran.

With each passing month, Leta grew heavier with child. Spending more time at Oriama's home and less time with Toran was a gradual change, but inevitable. The tentative bond the girls had formed with Toran, a bond Atha never really had, was fragile too. Being around their father rekindled their old natural bonds with him causing them to gravitate to the family 'visiting days.' Also, it was the time when they could see their brother who almost never stayed at their home any longer.

Leta's grudging initial acceptance of the edict leading to her pregnancy evolved as she accepted her husband's opposing views. The idea of further pairings with other men didn't sit well with the reunited couple. "I will carry no further babies unless they are yours, Oriama."

"That's your choice, my darling. I choose not to challenge their decision in the settlement, at least for the moment. I'm happy to hear you say that, though. I tried to honor my words, but it's been very difficult to cede you to him each night."

"That time is nearly over. He'll be gone from our lives soon enough. Can you be patient a little while longer?"

"I can if I'm nowhere near him. I think Atha's hostility is rubbing off on me. I should be a better role model for my son. Intolerance isn't a trait I want to see in him."

"Our son is a younger version of his father and I'm happy about that."

"Thank you, but the problem remains. We must both of us cope with the fact that not all situations we face in life are ones which we like. There can be legitimate opposing points of view. I have no better ideas to solve the difficult problems, so I must accept a plan I don't like. If the future demands I submit my daughters, I can't say I'll react well. It's a big issue because the growing group of men following me; they're adapting my resistance as their own. A schism is growing with two definite camps on opposite sides of the issue. I don't want it this way, but the situation is what it is."

"Your men aren't alone in that transformation. I'm finding it increasingly more difficult to be compliant with Toran. There's new tension and it's getting worse rapidly. The girls pick up on the discord and it's showing up in them acting out. I've talked with many other women who aren't enamored with what we're expected to do. Parting from husbands is not sitting well in most households. Seeing their husbands with other women is as galling to us as for the men. The distress you mentioned, it's common with the rest of us. There's no escape from the feeling that what we're doing is wrong."

"I know I shouldn't say this, but it makes me happy to hear you say that."

"Many women are considering going as a group to the council to say we'll no longer 'be with men' who're not our spouses after we're pregnant. There's no reason for continuing the unions. The edict is fulfilled at that point, so why can't we live with our husbands then?"

"That would be a good first step. This gestation period where I have to wait apart from you is a bad idea. My anger grows daily and I see it in the other men too. People who are forced to live apart, I think very few are happy with it, whether males or females."

"I think it was a tentative choice of an arrangement the council made, which I understand, but there was no provision to assess the results and make any changes."

"I've got a few tentative choices of my own I can make." He formed a fist. Leta chuckled and hugged him tightly.

"I love you so much, Oriama."

Atha had just arrived and smiled at his parents. "I've got a couple of tentative choices too, father." Brandishing his fists, they all laughed.

A month after their conversation, Leta gave birth to a son. Naming him Stora, she showed him to Toran, but immediately she returned to residing with her husband. With Toran no longer living in her house, Oriama vacated the temporary home provided by the council and took up residence with his wife. In a way, it was a challenge to the council as Leta would have been expected to make herself available to the next man in line for impregnation in the revolving system of reproductive diversifications. Oriama voiced no objections, but his actions spoke volumes. No one would be entering his house to tamper with his wife.

The defiant act initiated more such rebellions as more births occurred each husband in the settlement re-claimed his wife, effectively short circuiting the original plan.

The council called a meeting to discuss the matter. Every adult person attended and this time they were vocal. There would be no further silent acquiescence.

The settlement leader, a man uniformly respected began to speak. "I know the truth, my friends. It was a difficult matter before, and it's no less difficult now. Perhaps we should have done better discussing it then. We who made the decision weren't blind to the ramifications and the social stress it would cause. However, the problem is the same. This crop of new babies, I don't believe they're enough in numbers to solve the long term problem. I'm willing again to bear the burden of being vilified, like I'm promoting licentiousness and low moral character. You all know me better than that. I maintain it's a necessary evil with a community so small in numbers. These babies are the only way we can have a future. If someone has a better plan, we're all ears. The only compromise I can see is to continue with our cross breeding, though we can certainly change it to the impregnating act only without the men required to live with the women after it's done. Family structure is thereby maintained; the husband's raise the new babies as their own. What do you say, Oriama? Would you accept this for your wife, and would you become a sire with other women?"

"I don't want to be some pivotal figure influencing everyone else. I prefer each family make their own decisions to comply, or not."

"Non-compliance can't be an option for any person, at least not until we have a minimum number of babies from different father's to have a chance at genetic survival. Your contribution is as essential as any other man. As a settlement we chose to put moral niceties aside, not for any thrill of multiple unions, but for unavoidable necessity. Making those hard choices aren't something you can opt out of. Do you see?"

"I'm not looking to dispute with you, nor am I looking for special treatment. However, ignoring my moral compass, that's not so easy a task. It's a bad enough challenge for we adults, but the future you hold for my little daughters? How can I live with that? I'm their father and protector."

There was a strong reaction throughout the crowd, murmurs of support for Oriama. The leader was daunted.

Before he could speak in response, there was a sound in the distant sky. The crowd turned their heads to look and saw clouds roiling growing rapidly into a large scale storm front. Approaching rapidly, it mirrored nothing they'd experienced before in their time on the planet.

Loud booms of thunder echoed across the countryside, lightning flashed in bright jagged bolts, some touching the ground. The dark clouds evolved into multi-colors, roiling even more dangerously, growing to encompass the entire horizon. When the clouds moved to a point covering the sun, it became eerily dark. The onlookers were frightened, but frozen in place. Racing to their flimsy wooden dwellings didn't seem a protection against this massive weather front.

Oriama felt strangely. The power of the storm reverberated in his body, like the two were somehow linked together. Feeling invigorated and terrified simultaneously, there was a portentous aura to the moment that was lost on none of them.

As the storm came over top of the settlement, a blast of cool air swept through the crowd. It too was invigorating, like pure oxygen flooding their lungs. The people exclaimed simultaneously in awe at the sensation.

Frightening eruptions in the upper atmosphere rattled the ground, but the people remained captured in the overpowering event.

A blinding light pierced the dark clouds with a deep tone as suddenly Oriama began to glow.

Every mind received thoughts simultaneously from a new source, beings from a higher plane of existence. Oriama's mouth moved speaking in an unknown language to the settlers, but they understood the meaning of the words from the mental connections. "We are the Eviscoma."

"Oriama?" Leta asked in fear.

Turning his face, his eyes were aglow with near blinding light. "I was he, I am he, and I am also more. His death was a passage to a different existence. We Eviscoma no longer have corporeal forms, but here we've chosen that I share a new life with him. All that he was, I understand. We know your moral dilemma but we cannot participate in your choices. Oriama can only remain pure to the way. Though you feel you do what you must, he can't be a part of it. No Eviscoma can do moral wrongness, no matter the rationalization. His choices become my choices. Without me, he reverts back into the ground. Without him, I'm returned to my kind."

"What should we do?" asked the leader.

"We can't direct you about your life choices. You have free will to choose as you will."

"Are you saying we're wrong to interbreed, that it condemns us after life is over?"

"No."

The leader looked puzzled. "This is confusing what you say."

"Life is choices. Not every choice is a good one, yet sometimes difficult choices are necessary. It isn't the purpose of the Eviscoma to judge you or to interfere in your lives. You do what you feel you must. The same is true for us. Your fallen comrade fulfills a purpose for us which we cannot explain to you. Living amongst you, he's the same man he was, but simultaneously he coexists with us in a vital way. As I said, as a re-born shared entity he's more than he was but that doesn't mean he's a danger to you. With our connection and participation his standard for living can only be the strictures of the Eviscoma."

The audience of settlers were rapt and awed with the moment. The leader spoke again.

"Will you answer a question? How is it possible to bring him back from death?"

"There's a narrow window of three days after death to revive your bodies and still retain your souls, but only in this form where an Eviscoma joins with you to make the new hybrid being. It's possible for whom we've evolved into and the higher plane of existence where we reside. If we still had our former corporeal forms before our ascension, we'd be subject to the same limitations as you."

"Amazing, thank you for this gift. We'll honor your tenets, though we may need further guidance. Will you continue to communicate with us?"

"This audience can't be repeated. Oriama will have an inner template he will follow. Treat him as normal but give him latitude about controversial edicts. The Eviscoma wish you well and tell you do not fear death. What comes afterwards is nothing to fear. Goodbye."

Oriama ceased to glow and resumed his human countenance, blinking his eyes like he was coming out of a trance.

"Husband, are you aware of what happened?"

"Yes, I hope I didn't frighten you. I'm truly no threat to the community."

The settlers eyed him in silence, like he was a minor deity come amongst them.

Oriama looked at his wife. "Also, I speak truly when I say that I love and cherish you, Leta."

She hugged him, swept with the strong emotions of the moment, and her own feelings of love. Oriama took the hands of his precious little daughters to lead them away. They smiled at him, their Father in their hearts.

"I'll take my family and go to our home. Peace be with you all."

19.
Petal Infusion
Yasmin Khan

Attracting pollinators
fragrant colored corolla
wafting redolence in air
ribboning the wind...
wreathing an ambrosial
trail of opulent zephyr
floral envelopes scenting,
aromizing breath.

20.
Sensing Spring
A. J. Huffman

Seasonal rebirth.   The phoenix
rises in shades of green.   Leaves
and stems, reinforced by hibernation,
smile, re-introduce themselves, rainbow rations
for eyes starved by long months of white.

I. Touching Spring

Tickle of newborn grass on naked toes,
still damp with morning's mist.   Forceful whisp
of wind warming caterpillar's cocoon, waiting
to welcome first flutter of fledgling wings.   The gentle
tap of rain, hydrating kiss turning everything upward
towards gracious rays of sun.

II. Hearing Spring

Persistent chitter from nest resonates desperate
desire for food and mother's comforting presence
echoes across roofs, lawns, forest paths.   The next
generation of flight is lined up, mouths open,
demanding fuel.   Life's first lesson is accepted
as regurgitation, greedily swallowed without thought.
Excitement resounds, gains temperance, perceptible pitch
as they inch closer to take-off.   A vocal countdown
trails off to lone goodbye as feathers finally find wind.

III. Seeing Spring

Seeds split ground, miniature earthquakes across the yard,
shoot shafts that rise like giant arms busting through coffin's
lid. A slice of emerald radiates against the boring brown
of waking earth, reflecting hope of continuation. The first
is only the harbinger blade, carving the way for the rest of
the lawn. An icon of cycle, of birth and death
interlinked, it takes nourishment from an expanse
that seems almost absent, but soon will glow with being.

IV. Smelling Spring

Nature's aroma therapists have lifted their shutters, sent their
wares
to fill the world with wonder. Choruses of lilac and magnolia battle
for top spot, mingle magnificently against the wind. The goldenrod
will not
be out done, tickles nasal hairs until they turn away. *Aaachooo!*
The subtle struggle for attention, daisy, tulip, sunflower, all wait for
wandering
feet to stop, stoop, inhale their softer offerings. A calm rises,
echoes
across parks, lawns, enters windows left open for just this strain of
fevered smile.

V. Tasting Spring

Season of salads.   Greens flow straight from garden to bowl. Primal,
we feed from earth.   Carrots crunch, peas snap, both bathing mouth
in sweet freshness.   Hands drawn to bountiful branches, grab cherries
and pears, feed them to teeth all too eager to tear through tender skin.
Escaping drops of juice are retrieved by greedy tongue.   For dessert?
Vine-ripened strawberries, seed-studded pulp glazed into crust,
warmed and warming, filling stomachs that wish they could smile.

21.
Shades of Progression
A. J. Huffman

after *The Quiet Thunder*, artist Osnat Tzadok

Lavender sky leaks like soft eyes after pain.
Traces, barely perceived, hints of blue
that once was, run from the fray,
the anger that can no longer be contained.
Lone eruption flares, burning white,
electric.   Tendrils of fire, consume completely
before closing forever.   Unseen, residual thunder
rumbles for a while, eventually gets swallowed
by tomorrow's potential.

22.
Spring Ditty
Yasmin Khan

serenading dawn
twittering, chirping spring's rites~~
a fine canticle

arousing the day
from the slumber of night's sleep~~
dulcet orchestra

rhapsodizing birds
as they teach hatchlings to fly~~
on zephyr's wings

a mellifluous
exuberant rendition~~
nature's symphony

23.
Spring Enchantment
Yasmin Khan

beautiful little globules
silvery crystal droplets
Humming softly as they fall
gliding down gently

hummingbirds are frolicking
butterflies are flitting around
birds twittering and chirping
serenading joy

an ambrosial shower
a light indulgent sprinkling
moistening the balmy earth
a redolent dip.

24.
Spring Showers
Yasmin Khan

crystal droplets scintillate in balmy air
tumbling gently over upturned
trees and flowers, eagerly waiting
for the sprinkling, dancing precip.
slipping daintily into flowing streams
sliding over glistening rocks, mossy stones
splashing playfully
delighting ears with mellow refrain
joyfully heralding vivacity
vitality's continuance bestows liberally
streaming succulent enhancement
dewdrops effervesce on blossoms
birds sip driblets on leaves
foliage sparkles, a virginal lustre
luscious coverlet enwraps sensibilities
mellifluous clasping of nature
dulcet blessing from the heavens
coruscating liquid sunshine
deliquescent elixir rejuvenating.

25.
Spring Twilight
Yasmin Khan

Irises gleam
A moonbeam falls
Jasmin blooms

Scenting the air
Blossoms bare pale
And flare in gloam

Crepuscle fire
Sapphire bright
Desire ignite

26.
Subdivision Smackdown
Mary Ann Back

History is filled with bad ideas – the Edsel, lobotomies, and leisure suits spring quickly to mind. But the notion of building a Fourth-of-July float that represented all of Buckland Avenue was beyond comprehension.

East Buckland was nouveau riche, upscale and swanky with manicured lawns. West Buckland, beyond Baker Street, was nouveau po', a nightmarish minefield of lawn jockeys, flamingos, gnomes, and gazing balls all battling for world domination one yard at a time.

In the dog days of '62, I was a fifteen-year-old West Bucklander with a summer school project, courtesy of Mr. Willard, my social science teacher. He'd given me an incomplete in Anthropology. We were supposed to observe and document cultural based behaviors on film. He denounced my documentary "Movie Monsters: Shapeshifters of American Culture" as unadulterated rubbish and demanded a new "reality" based film. Failure to comply would turn my incomplete into an "F". I was dumbfounded. What phenomenon could possibly have had a greater impact on cultural behavior than monsters of the silver screen? I'd done enough fieldwork sitting in the Danbury Theatre, popcorn in hand, to know. I was struggling to find the right subject matter until I saw a poster for the Fourth-of-July parade. The wheels began to turn.

My film would depict the classical East meets West conflict, though any fool could see that the twain was never going to meet on Buckland Avenue. But no one listens to fifteen-year-olds, so I decided if I couldn't stop the madness, by God, I was going to film it. Mr. Willard would get reality. He should have been careful about what he wished for.

The neighborhood association decided each street would produce one float that displayed tableaus of the American lifestyle. The east Bucklanders, led by Mr. Willard and his wife Beverly, created a suburban Shangri-La on their half the float, with a z-brick wall, petunia beds, chaise lounges, and a charcoal grill; whereas the west side, with Butch and Tammy Hadley at the helm, went with a more rustic approach on their side, punctuated by hunting rifles, gun racks, and decapitated animal heads.

By nine o'clock on July 4th, the float parked at the corner of Buckland and Baker was piled high with Americana. Beverly wore her crisp white tennis dress, accessorizing with a Spaulding wooden racket. Mr. Willard climbed aboard in his Dennis the Menace apron carrying hot dogs and buns. Tammy joined the group in her little white shorts and matching silk head-scarf. Tension flared when Mr. Willard and Tammy made eye contact. Beverly bristled; her eyes flashed the words, 'white trash hussy!' It was common knowledge in our tiny little town that Mr. Willard had been diddling Tammy for years. Beverly did her best to hold her head high and ignore the melodrama. Tammy's hubby, Butch, sat on the floor of the float next to the gun rack, staring into space. He needed a beer.

The parade began at ten o'clock. Butch found the beer and returned to his trance; Mr. Willard grilled hot dogs and tossed them to the crowd. Beverly watched Tammy like a hawk. Tammy was waving to the crowd like a beauty queen, and with a throaty laugh, untied the scarf covering her long dark hair. The scarf wafted in the breeze and wrapped around Mr. Willard's head. He turned giving Tammy a playful wink. Tammy responded with an indiscreet squeeze of his ass.

Beverly backhanded her racket across the float, aiming for Tammy's face, but her stroke fell short and knocked over the grill. Hot embers landed on Mr. Willard's apron, setting him ablaze.

Dennis the Menace's face melted away, leaving behind a grizzly cartoon. Mr. Willard stopped, dropped, and rolled off the float, drawing panicked screams from the crowd. The toppled grill had scattered hot coals across the float; its plastic green turf melted, releasing noxious fumes. Ammunition from the gun racks exploded. Hysterical children flung themselves from the float. Beverly body-slammed Tammy and launched them both airborne. Butch cradled the beer cooler in his arms and hurtled over the blaze to safety.

The unmanned float blazed down the street obliterating everything in its path, eventually rolling to a smoldering stop after ramming into the back of a station wagon.

Mr. Willard, charred and shaken, stumbled into the street, scanning the carnage. He froze when he saw my camera and realized I'd filmed the most embarrassing moments of his life. I can still see him, as if in slow motion, lurching across the double yellow, a blood-curdling 'NOOOOO!' bursting from the depths of his lungs.

And that was a wrap. I had the power of the gods in my hands. The scent of an imminent "A" filled my nostrils.

That was forty-eight years ago. It was also the last time the subdivision asked Buckland Avenue to participate in the parade. The Bucklanders of '62 have all scattered to the winds. Beverly was committed to Longview Hospital for the criminally insane. It was all very hush-hush, something about her attempting to castrate men with her tennis racket. Mr. Willard ran off with Tammy, who then left him to marry a movie producer. They had a daughter who recently starred in the blockbuster porn flick "The Nymphs of Jersey Shores". After sobering up long enough to realize Tammy had left him, Butch found nirvana by turning his in-ground pool into a giant beer cooler. He had a Porta-Potty installed poolside and, as far as I know, neither he nor his lawn chair has moved since.

Disgraced and alone, Mr. Willard retired from teaching and went to live among the Oompa Loompas or some such tribe. I gave the film to him that night after the parade, and in return, he gave me my "A". I saw him burning something in his yard around midnight. I had to smile. Did he really believe I'd given him my only copy? I was young, but I wasn't stupid.

It's digitized now. Check it out on YouTube, "Subdivision Smack-Down: A Study in Human Behavior." It's had 1,352,417 hits. And most of them are from my Anthropology students.

27.
That Hole in the Sky
Cate Caldwell

"Is it just me," shouted Beth, half hanging outside the ice-cream van, "Or does the sky have a big hole in it?"

"It's a cloud," said Jeremy.

Beth dropped back inside. "You can't even see it."

Jeremy braked, stuck his head outside the window, and then turned back to Beth. "Yup. A cloud. Unless you're on drugs. Then it could be anything."

"They don't sell drugs at Home Depot, jerk face. Give me a Bomb Pop."

"Can you pay for it?" Jeremy asked, mostly joking.

"I would, but I spent all my money on duct tape," Beth said, holding up her bag.

"God, how many rolls did you buy? Ask dot com said it only takes two to make a dress."

"Yeah, but I needed a bunch of colors," said Beth. "And I need to make your suit."

Jeremy hit the brakes, hard. "I don't remember agreeing to wear a duct tape suit. Do you know how bad that's going to smell by the end of the night?"

"It's a homecoming dance, Jer. We'll be there for what, twenty minutes? Then we can come home and watch Kung Fu movies and eat ice cream."

"Then why are you going to all this effort?" Jeremy asked. "To impress people you don't like, who don't like you, for twenty minutes?"

"I like making things out of duct tape," Beth said, running her fingers through her blue hair. A high school junior, she was the only person in the whole small town with an "unnatural" hair color. Making art made her feel less alienated somehow, like she might just live long enough to leave.

"The how about making us a ship so we can sail on outta here?" Jeremy asked.

"That's next," Beth said.

Jeremy pulled up in front of Beth's house. "Later, lady," he said, kissing her on the cheek.

He was shy like that. Beth thought it was cute, but after four months of it, she was beginning to wonder if he was gay.

The door creaked as she elbowed her way in, hands full. The house was spartan. This meant it was small, had few furnishings and was falling apart. An out of place vanity with an enormous mirror took up half the living room. Beth's mother had inherited it, and it wouldn't fit in any other room. Beth had always hated it.

Her twelve-year-old sister Cass was sitting on the couch watching RoboCop and eating Crunchberries. Her unmanageable mop of dark brown curls had clearly yet to be washed or brushed.

"How many times have you seen that?" Beth demanded.

"As many as you," said Cass.

"Are you going to eat anything else for dinner?" asked Beth.

"Probably have another bowl, later," said Cass.

"Any word from mom?" asked Beth.

"What is this, the Spanish Inquisition? You want to know where she is, call her yourself," grumbled Cass, turning up the volume on ED 209, shooting up the board room.

Beth dumped her bag of duct tape with an unceremonious thud and went off to get her own bowl of nutritious sugary dinner.

Carrying the bowl of cereal with one hand, she swiped the bag off the coffee table and went to her room to start on her formal.

There were only five rolls of duct tape in it.

She stormed back into the living room. "Cass, dammit. You stole my pink. Give it back."

"I don't know what you're talking about," said Cass.

"Give me the pink or I'll come over there and shake you upside down," said Beth. She wasn't sure she could, Cass was as tall as she was now, but that wouldn't stop her from trying.

Cass sprang from the sofa, putting the coffee table between herself and Beth. Beth chased her. They ran around for a good five minutes until Beth caught Cass by her curls.

"Okay, fine," screeched Cass. Beth let go. Cass stepped back and hurled the tape at Beth, who reflexively ducked.

The tape flew across the room and crashed into the mirror on the vanity. Cracks spidered from the point of impact like an angry, bloodshot eye.

Cass and Beth looked at each other. Then they burst out laughing.

Her laugh turned into a strangled sound as she glimpsed a ghost-like tendril out of the corner of her eye.

Her head snapped toward the vanity.

"What's wrong with you?" Cass asked, still laughing. "You've always hated that thing."

"You didn't see that?" Beth asked.

"Are you on drugs?" Cass asked.

"Why does everyone keep asking me that?" Beth demanded.

But then, eight translucent tentacles reached out from the cracks in the mirror like creepy, slimy snail tails. They grabbed Cass by her hair, making the already unruly mass writhe like a gorgon. She shrieked loud and long enough to send a banshee fleeing.

Beth tried to slice through the tentacles with her sewing scissors, but they were ghostly and it had no effect. In desperation, she grabbed the roll of pink duct tape. She leapt to the mirror and slapped on a long, diagonal strip like a police line.

As she had hoped, the tentacles could not pass through the tape. One disentangled itself from Cass' hair to come after Beth, but she held out the sticky side. The tentacle slapped on and got stuck like a child's tongue on a winter streetlamp.

Frantic, she laid strip after strip of pink duct tape across the mirror until it was entirely covered. After several minutes, the thrashing from behind the mirror subsided.

"It looks a lot better, now," said Cass. "Sorry I ruined your dress."

"No worries," said Beth. "My heart really isn't in it. Jeremy would rather come over here."

"I think your boyfriend is gay," said Cass.

"I know," said Beth.

"What are you going to do with the rest of the tape?" asked Cass.

"Save it," said Beth. "I might need to fix that hole in the sky."

28.
The Parade
Nancy Cole Silverman

The fact that Second Lieutenant Adrian Camacho's alarm didn't wake him on the morning of the big parade should have been his first sign that things weren't going to go as planned that day. He was up before the first signs of yellow daylight shred like broken glass across the dry desert floor. Shaken from his dream with the elders, he pulled the plug on the annoying ticking clock, got up, went to the open window and waited for the sun to rise. An early morning breeze lightly bathed his brown skin and announced a new day followed by the faint cooing of mourning doves and the rustling of tree branches as they stretched to greet the warming sun. Somewhere in the background he could hear the faint sound of their drums. He knew they would not welcome the day's activities.

The young lieutenant's second sign that things weren't proceeding according to plan came the minute he walked through the doors of his office.

"The Chamber of Commerce called. The PA system's not functioning. You're going to have to use a bullhorn to start." Lieutenant Camacho's assistant, a pert, blue eyed blonde, handed him a memo. "They sent over a list of the parade entries. You might want to look through these."

Adrian sipped his coffee, the acid in his stomach already beginning to bubble up as he glanced through the descriptions for the Extraterrestrial Day Parade, an annual celebration in recognition of the mysterious Roswell UFO Incident of 1947. An odd assortment of kiddie carts, pony rides and dog walkers mixed in between a half dozen old jalopies, designed to carry today's VIP's – the mayor and his wife, the local sheriff and the president of the

Chamber of Commerce - all decorated up with streamers and American flags.

"This it?" He asked.

"You might want to see this." His assistant shoved an eight and a half by eleven photo into his hand and smirked. "It's from last year. Can you believe people actually think this is real?" He glanced at a picture of a bamboo jail with four bug-eyed, emaciated looking aliens peering back at him and grimaced.

As the area's lowest ranking Public Affair's Officer, Lieutenant Camacho, was assigned as the liaison-on-loan from the US Air Force to Roswell's local Chamber of Commerce. His purpose was to field difficult questions and quell any public fears that aliens might be lurking in their midst.

In truth, Adrian thought, the event was little more than an outreach campaign – a government attempt to cover up the seriousness of Roswell's sightings with all the frivolity of a poor man's Mardi Gras. An annual street fair, orchestrated by the state legislature, an attempt to poke fun at what the government hoped to pass off as trivial UFO sightings; reclassifying them as mistaken identities of silver lined weather balloons and unspecified Air Force test-craft.

Whatever the reason, Lieutenant Camacho's job was to put a face on the parade – the happy smiling face of certainty - that denied any knowledge of UFOs or space aliens, despite his own personal beliefs. As a boy he'd been taught of his ancestry, about the cave dwellings, the etchings of star people on their walls and their connections to the extraterrestrials. His grandfather had shown him the large circles in the land telling him they were space coordinates to those from the worlds beyond.

Whether it was the faint sound of the drums or the vibration from his dream still pounding in his ears as he climbed the steps to

the podium, he wasn't sure.   He paused and scanned the horizon.
Above him, skies like thin milk stood empty.   Beneath him the
dusty street now cleared for the parade was jammed on either side
with city folk and day trippers.   Costumed aliens stood two and
three deep, the sunlight catching the refection from their silvered
swords and bobbing antennas.   But it was the small group of elders,
barely visible through the haze, sitting on lawn chairs apart from
the group that worried him.

     "You ready, Lieutenant?" The Master of Ceremonies
nodded to him and smiled.   Today's fly-by was to be an
unprecedented surprise.   "Call in your birds."

     Lieutenant Camacho keyed the command into his cellphone
and within minutes the deep, dark roar of the US Air Force
Thunderbirds shook the air.   Before they were even visible, the
crowd could hear the screaming of their engines, coming closer.

     "Look! Look, there they are!"

     Shrieks, then hands, arms and fingers like directional rods
pointed upward.   Faces turned, heads followed, necks cranked
each trying to catch the F-16s as they streaked low in formation
over the parade route at speeds too fast to clock.   Then bursting
up, straight up into the sky like a starburst, each jet broke away in a
different direction. It was awesome.

     "Over there!"

     "They're coming back! Look!"

     Just as planned they returned, diving from heights high
above the crowd and in death defying formation.   But this time, as
they swept past the crowd every other plane, suddenly flipped and
flew upside down.   Their precision and speed was stupefying.   The
crowd cheered. The US Air Force had triumphed and doing a final
pass above the crowd tipped their wings then disappeared into the
sky as quickly as they had come.

Lieutenant Camacho turned his attention back to the parade route. A small wired haired terrier had broken loose from the crowd and was running up the street, barking at the sky, chasing after the departed jet jockeys.

The crowd laughed, and then suddenly stopped.

In the sky above lights appeared. Like a blast from a shot gun, thousands of tiny white glowing specs, bright and intense, pulsated then swept towards the crowd. People shielded their eyes and looked away and as they did, large disc shaped objects appeared and their lights dimmed, but not their show.

It was as though the aliens had been challenged. And the people who were there will tell you they will never forget. They hovered, they swooped, and they swarmed in formation. Then they left, quickly as they came. It was as though they wanted us to know. They are here and they are waiting.

29.
To Dye For
Chloe Vider

They came out of the dye transformed
little white orbs no longer pure
   she wished she could
change color so quickly
become a chameleon
dart from prey through camouflage
and diversion
but alas, she was no Easter egg.

Just a frumpy housewife
dreams washed down the drain
with red hair dye
a jar of sea glass on the windowsill
all that remains
of her youth

she traces her lips with red pencil
screams into a full sink
emerges,
edges blurred
not a beautiful white orb turning color
but complete disarray
dripping dye down her white gown
   losing hope in any last chances for
 transformation.

30.
Traveler
Stanley Noah

My dog howls at the moon while I'm beside the camp fire.   He
comes over and tells me this story like an old pal, as to why dogs
howl in the night. Something about paranormal activity. And not
knowing exactly how he came to earth against his own free will.
He said, forced by humans. Though I find
it strange, my dog is good at tricks. Some I never taught him. He
said dogs are not really howling at the moon like humans believed.
But it's like a kind of early voice mail searching, reaching back
somewhere. He said I won't believe any of this stuff
by morning.   It would sound too fantastic, too distasteful as if again
he was telling
me about slavery or another notorious genocide my mind couldn't
lift.

31.
Walking Through, Riding Home
Stanley Noah

It all started one morning a few years ago.

Left the

house, down porch steps, across the lawn to the side
walk.   But
this was a somewhere different day.   One like I
had never seen.   I could smell wood
and coal burning.

   And all the houses had chimneys.   Suddenly,
I noticed walking forward
                was also like walking backward in time.
Children playing
roll-the-ring. A forgotten game. All women had long hair,

long dresses, sun hats as if they were characters right
out of Gone With The Wind.
                       Then a breath of horses could
be felt on my back shoulder. A big mare coaxing me to
ride
pass barns, haystacks, rolls of king cotton and down by the
silver river, old man river, the Mississippi.
                            And on board a
noisy steam boat toward
home.

                            Every minute of it like another
life like another memory, traveling like a trunk
full of letters with dried pressed flowers between pages,

   taken to an attic beside a small window that never forgets.

32.
What Will You Have?
Chloe Vider

"Put a pin in it"
he said as he tossed back another vodka tonic,
her lacquered nails danced across the bar top
raindrops pelting a swimming a pool,
disappearing into vast puddles
absorbing sweat and condensation,
powdered sugar on top.

Neon pink streaks in the sky
reminded him of lines of grease in a frying pan.
There was nothing beautiful in leftovers.

Training wheels anchored tight
like a first job
or a bachelor's degree,
sharks circling their prey
an interview gone awry
nothing comes from such carnage

"A vodka martini with a twist,"
she says, likes she's ordering
a night of passion in the bedroom
and cuff links
by the bathroom sink
but really she just ordered
a headache, a loose bra, and mascara marks
strewn across her face like scars from a battle.

The bartender collects their isolation like tips in a jar
and squirrels them away for future use
like that divorcee he served six rounds and

the shadow of tomorrow,
he goes home and wonders
"am I a salesman, a doctor, or a priest?"
but in the end the man who pours the drinks
 is all three
or when the glass empties,
he is none.

Contributing Authors

A.J. Huffman

A. J. Huffman

Where are you from?
Ormond Beach, Florida

When and why did you begin writing?
Writing always just kind of came naturally to me. I wrote my first short story in grade school. It was about living in a yellow submarine with my pet fish. And I, of course, I wrote poetry in high school. But I didn't actually start taking my writing seriously until I got to college.

What would you say is your most interesting writing quirk?
I still prefer to write with a pen on paper. My writing friends think I'm nuts. They are all die-hard type straight to the screen computer writers.

What do you like to do when you're not writing?
Dude! I live in Florida! I'm at the beach!

As a child, what did you want to do when you grew up?
When I was a little girl I wanted to be a fashion designer. I was a total girly girl. I loved clothes and dresses and shoes. Oh wait, I still do, I just can't sew.

Chloe Viner

Chloe Viner

Where are you from?
I grew up in New Orleans and Boston and currently live in Vermont with my husband Shane and our rescue pets Haley (dog) and Milo (cat.)

When and why did you begin writing?
When I was nine a good friend of mine passed away and I wrote my first poem to read at his memorial service.

What do you like to do when you're not writing?
Read, rescue animals, work to protect the environment, camp, hike, and sit on our balcony that overlooks the green mountains.

As a child, what did you want to do when you grew up?
I wanted to save the tropical rainforest and animals.

Dennis K. Hausker

Dennis K. Hausker

Where are you from?
I was born in Yale, Michigan, the middle child of five. We reside in Macomb, but with my wife being from Maine, she would move back there "in a New York minute," to use her words.

When and why did you begin writing?
I dabbled with writing starting in my twenties, but my employments were consuming, so I never accomplished much as a write back then. After retirement, I finally had time and have been writing for 5-6 years, mostly epic fantasy. I have double digit books and anthologies on the market currently. I write because I enjoy it, I find it fun and I've been blessed that I never have writer's block. My stories just flow onto the pages.

What would you say is your most interesting writing quirk?
I'd say my writing goals. I hope to differentiate my writing from usual ruts. In every story, I look to evoke the reader's feelings, whether with action driven story lines, shocking plot twists, considerable bombs I drop on the reader, and in particular including compelling social issues partially as a means that we look at the reality of who we are, rather than the façade we pretend to be.

What do you like to do when you're not writing?
I'm a sports fanatic, particularly for my alma mater, Michigan State University. Secondly, we like to travel on vacations.

As a child, what did you want to do when you grew up?
At age 66, that was a long time ago. I didn't aspire to be President. I think I briefly had some thoughts about music and sports. I was actually a 'music major' at MSU for a single quarter before I realized there are other better French Horn players. The money was elsewhere. Oh well.

Dennis Klotz

Dennis Klotz

Where are you from?
Dearborn Heights, MI.

When and why did you begin writing?
I started writing seriously when I was twenty-one. I was inspired by short stories and how challenging they are to write well. As difficult as they are to write, they have the potential to pack a real emotional punch and that's what I want to do; to move people emotionally with my stories.

What would you say is your most interesting writing quirk?
I always start with the ending in mind because I feel even good stories lose their power without a solid ending.

What do you like to do when you're not writing?
Most of the time I read, play guitar, write music, cook, and study ways to better myself.

As a child, what did you want to do when you grew up?
I wanted to be a pirate, then a fire fighter, and then a rock star.

Evelyn Zimmer

Evelyn Zimmer

Where are you from?
Waterford, Michigan, born and raised.

When and why did you begin writing?
I've always had a need to write. It brings me joy to put words to paper. To preserve the stories of my imagination makes room for new stories!

What would you say is your most interesting writing quirk?
Arguing with the characters in my head and trying to convince them I know better than they.

What do you like to do when you're not writing?
Read, Read, Research, Read some more

As a child, what did you want to do when you grew up?
When in high school, I wanted to be an attorney, an accountant, an archeologist, an author... looking at this list, it matches my A-type personality rather well.

Heather Moser

Heather Moser

Where are you from?
A small town in Ohio.

When and why did you begin writing?
I began writing poetry when I was a teenager in an attempt to deal with difficult emotions. I decided to start with poetry because my Dad writes love poems to my mother, and I admire that kind of affection. I have just started writing short stories within the last year.

What would you say is your most interesting writing quirk?
I save every version of and edit to my poetry I have ever written. I just cannot bring myself to discard my original poems because every word is deliberately chosen to capture a moment in time.

What do you like to do when you're not writing?
I love spending time with my family and researching anything related to ancient Rome.

As a child, what did you want to do when you grew up?
When I was a small child, a paleontologist. As an older child into early high school years, an astronomer. By my sophomore year of high school, I wanted to be a classicist.

Jay Dardes

Jay Dardes

Where are you from?
Northwestern Pensylvania; I live on twenty-two wooded acres with my wife, Elaine, and my dog, Gretel.

When and why did you begin writing?
Started when I was about 5 probably because my father, my hero, was a freelance writer.

What would you say is your most interesting writing quirk?
I avoid writing so thoroughly that I haven't developed any quirks.

What do you like to do when you're not writing?
Travel, read, play with my dog, activities with my wife. I am a retired psychotherapist and I always enjoyed that.

As a child, what did you want to do when you grew up?
A Cowboy.

Jessica Malen

Jessica Malen

Where are you from?
Detroit, MI

When and why did you begin writing?
I began writing at about ten years of age. I think it has always been a form of escape for me.

What would you say is your most interesting writing quirk?
I really need silence or soft classical music to be playing for me to write. I can't have noise.

What do you like to do when you're not writing?
I enjoy cooking a lot, hanging out with my friends and going to concerts. I am really into Pilates as well. Exercising and taking care of myself mentally and physically is very important to me. I also love to travel!

As a child, what did you want to do when you grew up?
I wanted to be a vampire at the age of five. But I have always wanted to own my own café or vineyard.

Mark Hudson

Mark Hudson

Where are you from?
Evanston, Illinois

When and why did you begin writing?
I went to Columbia College in Chicago to study animation, because I'm an artist, but found It complicated, so I switched my major to fiction writing. I'm better at writing poetry Than fiction, but do write stories when they come to me.

What would you say is your most interesting writing quirk?
My most interesting writing quirk is I don't know what a quirk is. And you can print that. Might as well add a little humor.

What do you like to do when you're not writing?
I also draw, taking an art class at Noyes art center and a private portraiture class.

As a child, what did you want to do when you grew up?
My first goal was to be a garbage man. But then I didn't do good in high school, and ended Up with a lot of jobs dealing with taking out trash. Many artists I know had mundane jobs Before they got their art education, and you appreciate being able to write and do art When you've had lousy jobs.

Mary Ann Back

Mary Ann Back

Where are you from?
Mason, Ohio.

When and why did you begin writing?
My eighth-grade English teacher asked us to write a story. I fell in love with writing right then and there.

What would you say is your most interesting writing quirk?
I have a writing room that is decorated like a scene from a horror movie. It has black lace curtains, skeletons, Day of the Dead memorabilia, a stuffed raven, and even a chair with a purple velvet coffin back!

What do you like to do when you're not writing?
I love to run away for girl's weekends with my friends when I get the chance.

As a child, what did you want to do when you grew up?
I wanted to be a stay at home mommy and a nurse. So, naturally, I've worked my entire life and probably couldn't pass a chemistry test to save my soul. By the time I was in eighth grade, I knew I really wanted to be a writer.

Nancy Cole Silverman

Nancy Cole Silverman

Where are you from?
I was born in Seattle, Washington, but I grew up in the southwest and much later moved to Los Angeles, California.

When and why did you begin writing?
I started writing in the second grade. I don't think I had much to say back then, and I certainly struggled with the tools of the trade, but I was determined. As a kid I'd start my own newspapers, write short stories and spent a lot of time in my tree house reading and imagining I was on a space ship. One day, I knew I wanted to grow up be a great writer, in the meantime, I was just telling stories. It wasn't until I retired from twenty-five year in radio – where I wrote commercial copy, news stories and station promos – that I was able to sit down and really do what I wanted, write fiction.

What would you say is your most interesting writing quirk?
I believe turquois is a stone of communication. I have a ring I was given a long time ago that has very sentimental value to me and I like to wear it when I working on certain stories. I also have a clown doll that is very similar to a toy clown I received from my grandmother when I was a small child. I like to think she a guardian angel and watching over me while I write. I keep that on my desk to remind me of her presence.

What do you like to do when you're not writing?
I'm a big reader. I love to study how other authors have created their stories. If I'm not writing and reading, I love hiking and walking with my dogs. Animals are a big part of my life. I think they're our guides.

As a child, what did you want to do when you grew up?
I always wanted to be a writer. I was drawn to news when I was young and graduated college with a degree in broadcast journalism.

Sean McCarthy

Sean McCarthy

Where are you from?
Mansfield, Massachusetts—south of Boston.

When and why did you begin writing?
Well, I used to write dialogues in junior high school that often landed me on office detention, but it wasn't until the spring semester my senior year of college—I was a psychology major—when I took a creative course and it hit me. I had taken the wrong major!

What would you say is your most interesting writing quirk?
Once I stop procrastinating and open the page I can usually get into the zone—detaching myself from everything around me—in two minutes or less. And sometimes I speak my dialogue as I'm writing it.

What do you like to do when you're not writing?
I like to spend time with my wife and kids (I have a bunch of them), run, lift weights, canoe, go to Patriots' games, read, drink beer and wine and smoke cigars—but I don't let my kids smoke the cigars.

As a child, what did you want to do when you grew up?
When I was small I wanted to be a cartoonist, then I suppose I went through a phase where I wanted to be Clint Eastwood, and by the time college came around I wanted to be a psychologist. And now, of course, I'm none of the three.

Stanley Noah

Stanley Noah

Where are you from?
Dallas, Texas.

When and why did you begin writing?
2000 – Because I feel like I have something to say.

What would you say is your most interesting writing quirk?
Writing somewhere between realism and fiction.

What do you like to do when you're not writing?
Watching old black and white movies, and drinking gallons of coffee.

As a child, what did you want to do when you grew up?
A Professional Wrestler.

Yasmin Khan

Yasmin Khan

Where are you from?
Mumbai, India

When and why did you begin writing?
When I was barely four years old, the love of writing overcame my inhibitions of vocal speech and I was
very happy to put pen to paper.

What would you say is your most interesting writing quirk?
Thoughts and words keep shouting out in my mind , heart and my spirit keeps the soul searching .

What do you like to do when you're not writing?
I like to involve myself in the fragrance of cooking. nature thrills me no end and inspires me to boundless aspirations.

As a child, what did you want to do when you grew up?
I always wanted to be a writer, a poet and master all the words.

www.ingramcontent.com/pod-product-compliance
Lightning Source LLC
Chambersburg PA
CBHW070016260626
47159CB00005B/1827